OUT TO GET YOU

13 TALES OF WEIRDNESS AND WOE

by
JOSH ALLEN illustrated by
SARAH J. COLEMAN

HOLIDAY HOUSE · NEW YORK

"Vanishers" was originally published in
Cricket magazine in October 2016.

Library of Congress Cataloging-in-Publication Data

Names: Allen, Josh, author. | Coleman, Sarah J., illustrator.
Title: Out to get you : 13 tales of weirdness and woe / by Josh Allen ;
illustrated by Sarah J. Coleman.
Description: First edition. | New York : Holiday House, [2019]
Summary: A collection of thirteen short stories that reveal scary
secrets lurking in everyday objects.
Identifiers: LCCN 2018060602 | ISBN 9780823443666 (hardback)
Subjects: LCSH: Horror tales, American. | Children's stories, American.
CYAC: Horror stories. | Short stories. | BISAC: JUVENILE FICTION
Horror & Ghost Stories. | JUVENILE FICTION / Short Stories.
Classification: LCC PZ7.1.A4387 Ou 2019 | DDC [Fic]—dc23
LC record available at https://lccn.loc.gov/2018060602

DEDICATED TO
CARTER, TAYLOR,
MALLORY, AND WYATT.
AND TO SUZY.
ALWAYS.

CONTENTS

two
days
left

VANISHERS

THEY were best friends named Jacob and Jakob, and they lived next door to each other. Over the years, they'd built snow forts together and leaped off backyard sheds together, and one summer, they'd even broken their left wrists together in a freak trampoline accident.

At the end of fifth grade, they'd developed crushes on the same girl together—Bethany Miller, a black-haired beauty who could pitch a baseball so fast not even the eighth-grade boys could hit it. Neither of the boys did a thing about his crush, though, because neither was willing to risk losing their friendship—not even for Bethany Miller.

Jacob with a C. Jakob with a *K*. That's what people called them. Since they even looked alike—each had the same shaggy haircut, the same lanky walk, the same light freckles—if you wanted one of them, you just called out, "Hey, Jakob with a *K*," and waited to see which boy looked up.

"You need more friends," their parents sometimes told them. "This is getting weird."

But why, Jacob thought, should he make more friends when he had Jakob? And why, Jakob thought, should he make more friends with Jacob around?

One late October afternoon, when the last bell had rung and another day of sixth grade was finally over, Jacob and

Jakob met by the large maple tree to begin the walk home. They set out slowly, ambling along as clouds whirled and a light wind blew.

"Balotobob?" Jacob asked. The boys had their own language. They'd decided they needed one when a note they'd been passing in Social Studies last year had been confiscated and read aloud. *Balotobob?* meant *How are you?*

"Blapo," Jakob replied. *Good.* "Except I have to write a story for Ms. Jenkins's class tonight. A whole story with characters and a plot and everything."

The wind picked up, and they zipped their jackets against the chill.

"You hate writing," Jacob said. "If you want, I'll help you."

"Skolototh!" *Awesome!*

At the edge of the schoolyard, they pressed the button to cross Westover Street, and a streak of lightning flashed in the distance. A storm was coming.

"Well," Jacob said. "What does your story have to be about?"

"It can be about anything. But it has to be at least three full pages."

"You could make it a creepy story."

"A creepy story?" Jakob said. "You mean, like, with a monster?"

"Chellitarb," Jacob said. *Totally.* As he said this, the clouds thickened and swirled, and the afternoon's colors faded. Even the boys' faces paled in the changing light, taking on the faint yellow tint of old newspapers.

"That could work." Jakob nodded. "That could be cool." Cars waited as the boys crossed the street and stepped onto a leaf-covered sidewalk. Dried leaves crunched under their feet. "I watched a TV show last night about zombies. I could write about zombies."

Jacob let out a little puff of air. "No way!" he said. "Anything but zombies. They used to be creepy, like, a long time ago, but they're, like, all over the place now. There are zombie movies and zombie video games. There's even a zombie emoji." Jacob pulled out his phone, swiped a few times, and showed Jakob the green-gray zombie face on the screen. "Last week my mom bought some Halloween cereal, and it had zombie-head marshmallows in it."

"Yeah," Jakob agreed. "I guess you're right."

"You should make up a new kind of monster," Jacob said. In the distance lightning flashed, and the boys stopped to count for the thunder. After three seconds, it rumbled.

"A new kind of monster?" Jakob said. "Like what?"

Jacob stroked his chin, the way people did in movies when they were thinking. The boys rounded the corner and passed Nielsen's Drugstore. A faded sign in the window showed a smiling woman holding a yellow bottle of laundry detergent. Across the top the sign said, SPOT-B-GONE MAKES STAINS VANISH!

"Makes stains vanish," Jacob said, and pointed. "You could call your monsters the Vanishers."

"The Vanishers?" The wind hissed. Dried leaves skittered along the sidewalk. "What are Vanishers?"

"I'm not sure yet," said Jacob.

The boys turned off the main road and into their neighborhood. They walked quietly for a minute.

"These Vanishers are creepy though, right?" Jakob said. It was growing cold, and the boys shoved their hands into their pockets.

"Oh, they're plenty creepy. They're klotman creepy." *Klotman* meant something so strange and weird as to be almost unreal. "Just you wait."

They rounded another corner and walked in silence for a few minutes more.

"I've got it," Jacob said. "I know what Vanishers do."

"Let me guess," Jakob said. "They kill you. That's what all monsters do. Kill you."

"Not Vanishers," said Jacob. "Vanishers are different. They aren't murderers. Not really. They don't kill you. Instead, what they do is, they *vanish* you."

The clouds grew darker and thicker still, and by now the boys' faces appeared faint and ghostly.

"Vanishers wipe you out," Jacob said. "They erase you, like off a chalkboard. If the Vanishers set out to get you, they just get you, and there's nothing you can do about it. You'll be walking down the street one day, and all at once they'll zero in on you, and you'll get strange and milky, like a crystal ball. And then, little by little, you'll just fade away."

The first drops of rain fell. The boys paused to put their hoods up, and they cinched the strings tight around their faces.

"So you just disappear one day? And your parents and everyone have to wonder what happened to you?" Jakob said. "Like they do when someone goes missing on TV?" Jakob's voice came out soft and muffled through his hood and the wind and the rain. "That's a little scary, I guess, but it's not *that* scary. It's mostly sad."

"Well, it's worse than that," said Jacob. The boys walked with their heads down, braced against the weather. They turned onto their street. "Because when the Vanishers get you, you don't disappear from right now. You disappear from *forever*. Your birthdays. Your learning to walk. Everything. It's like none of it ever happened. No one remembers any of it. No one remembers you. You're *vanished*. You're erased. From *everywhere*."

A gust of wind bent the trees along the sidewalk.

The boys' homes came into view. Jacob's mother was out front in a long black coat, dragging a brown garbage bin in from the curb despite the wind and rain.

"Can you fight the Vanishers?" Jakob asked. "Can you outrun them?"

"No way!" Jacob hunched his shoulders as he reached his driveway, where he'd peel off and Jakob would keep going for one more house. "Vanishers don't even have bodies. They just exist, like, everywhere at once. In the light and the air and everywhere." He waved one hand in the damp air around him. "When they decide to get you, you're just gone. There's nothing you can do."

His mother pulled the garbage bin into the open garage. The bin rattled and slid. She looked up, rainwater dripping down her face.

"Who are you talking to?" she said.

Jacob pointed to his side. "I'm talking to . . ."

He stopped. He'd been telling a story, hadn't he? To someone? Talking about the Vanishers? The air around him felt heavy and cold, and he shivered. He turned in a full circle.

No one was there.

He looked to the gray brick house next door. There was a name he tried to call to mind. It had something to do with the letter *K*.

Kevin? Kacey? Kyle?

He shook his head.

"No one," he said. "I guess I was just talking to myself."

NINE LIVES
1 2 3 4 5 7 8 9

L ET me tell you something. There's a huge difference between cats and kittens. I noticed it years ago, back when I was still in pigtails and training wheels.

To start, kittens are way cuter. Their bodies haven't really grown to match the size of their heads, so they have these huge faces. I know that sounds weird, but trust me, it's super-adorable. And it gives kittens these big look-at-me eyes.

Plus, kittens will sit in your lap and let you pet them. At least Licorice always did. Licorice was the kitten Mom got me for my seventh birthday. He was covered in black fur—his face, his back, his legs—all black. That's why I named him Licorice.

Another thing that makes kittens so much better than cats is that kittens are unbelievably soft—their ears especially. I used to sit with Licorice in front of the TV and just fondle his velvety ears between my fingers and thumb. I could have done that all day. And Licorice would have let me, too.

But cats are nothing like kittens. *Nothing.*

Cats, if you want to know the truth, are kind of the worst.

Take Licorice. Once he grew up, he totally changed. He got big and kind of snobby, and he didn't want to sit in my lap anymore. He would, for a second, if I hoisted him up and made him, but once I got settled, he'd wriggle, jump off my lap, and prowl around the hallway instead.

That's what Licorice spent most of his time doing—prowling. Around the house, the yard, the neighborhood.

Once he became a cat, it was like he didn't care that I existed anymore.

And that wasn't even the worst thing about Licorice.

The worst thing was that he never learned to use the litter box. I could forgive that in Licorice the Kitten. I mean, if a cute kitten piddles on the floor once in a while and you have to clean it up, well, okay. But when Licorice the Full-Grown Cat did it, it felt different.

I guess Licorice tried. I mean, he actually did his business standing in the litter box. The problem was that his back end would always dangle over the edge, and the mess would plop down on the kitchen floor.

It drove Mom nuts. She'd come in from the garage holding a bag of groceries and see a pile of...well...you know, on her newly mopped kitchen floor, and she'd kind of lose it.

"Licorice!" she'd say. "Licorice! Oh, why do we even have a stupid cat?" Then she'd track down Licorice, drag him over to the pile, and say, "No, Licorice! No!"

I think she was trying to train him, like a dog.

It went on like this for years, and each time Licorice defiled the floor, Mom seemed to grow less patient.

"Cats are the worst," she said once while she mopped up a puddle.

"When Licorice dies, we're never getting another cat," she said another time. "Never."

And then one day she said, "I hate that cat." And I think she meant it. I really do.

A few weeks later, she walked into the kitchen one morning, still groggy-eyed and barefoot, and she stepped right into Licorice's latest delivery.

Squish!

"Licorice!" she said, and I could tell from her voice—how loud and high-pitched it was—that something in her had snapped.

She hopped over to Licorice on one foot, since her other foot was covered in you-know-what. She grabbed Licorice by the fur on the back of his neck and lifted him up. He didn't even squirm. He just hung there.

"Miranda, get my keys!" Mom called, still hopping on one foot. "And get in the car!"

Her face turned bright red, and she was shaking the way she does when I go a week without cleaning my room.

I grabbed her keys off the hook by the door and buckled into the passenger seat while Mom flung Licorice into the back of the car. He jumped up onto the back seat and started prowling around.

Mom backed out of the driveway.

"Three miles," she said under her breath. "That should be enough."

A hot hole opened up inside me. "Um, Mom," I said, but Mom raised one finger and shushed me.

She turned left onto Birch Bark Drive and made a right onto Harrison. She drove for a while, zipping around corners, and sometimes, out of the blue, she'd flip a U-turn and head in the opposite direction. I think she was trying to confuse Licorice, to get him good and lost.

Finally she pulled over at a farmer's cornfield.

She jumped out, not even bothering to turn off the car, and she swung open the back door.

I knew what Mom was going to do, but I didn't say anything. The hot hole in my chest opened up even further, and to tell you the truth, I was kind of thinking about how cats aren't kittens.

"Out!" Mom said, but Licorice just looked at her with his yellow-green eyes.

"Cat!" she said, not using Licorice's name. "Get out!" Again, Licorice just stared, so Mom leaned in and grabbed him. Then she tossed him toward the cornstalks. He twisted in the air and landed on his feet. Of course.

Licorice looked up. He took about two steps toward the car, but Mom said, "No!" Licorice froze. I rolled down the window.

Was Mom really going to do this?

At the side of the road, Mom waved her arms.

"Shoo!" she said. "Scat! Scram!" Then she got back in the car and slammed the door.

I opened my mouth, but Mom looked at me and said, "Not now, Miranda." So I closed it.

That's when the hot hole in my chest really started to burn. I began sweating a little, but still, I didn't say anything.

Maybe I should have.

Before I could think about it, Mom drove off. Behind us, Licorice stood by the side of the road. He tilted his head to one side, but he didn't run after us.

"Well," Mom said. "I'm glad that's over with."

She switched on the radio, but she must have noticed my face because she said, "Don't worry, Miranda." And then she said, "Licorice will be fine. Cats have nine lives."

I didn't answer her.

I didn't even speak.

⸺ ⸻

When we pulled into the driveway, believe it or not, there was a cat sitting on our front porch—a stray.

It was an orange cat. It was whisper thin and had a notch in its ear, and its fur was so sparse on one side you could see pale skin underneath.

"Not another one." Mom pointed at me. "Get rid of it, Miranda."

I got out of the car and walked to the porch. Mom went inside, and I waved my arms at the cat, like Mom had at Licorice.

"Shoo," I said, but I didn't scream it. I couldn't. I was

thinking about Licorice at the side of the road, so I only whispered.

"Scat," I said, but the word barely came out.

The orange cat didn't move. It tilted its head to one side. I stomped my foot against the sidewalk. I clapped my hands, but the cat stayed put. That was when I noticed it was missing an eye—its left one. The skin around where the eye should have been was pink and raw-looking, like the eye had only been gone a few days.

That orange cat just stood there on my porch—not moving, not leaving. It stared at me with its one good eye.

Get out of here, I tried to say but couldn't.

I don't know how long I stood there, getting stared down by a one-eyed cat. Maybe a few minutes. But I needed to get ready for school, so finally I stepped over the cat and went inside.

Half an hour later, when I opened the door carrying my lunch and my backpack, the cat was there, in the exact same place on our porch. It sat statue-still, like its one eye hadn't even blinked.

And there was something else. Something worse.

The one-eyed cat wasn't alone anymore.

It'd been joined by two more cats. They were just as thin, and they looked just as roughed-up. One of them had only three legs. The other had only half a tail. They looked at me together, and my neck hairs prickled.

I stepped out and closed the door, but the cats didn't move. They just kept staring. I had to tiptoe past them to get down the porch stairs.

As I headed to school, the cats finally shifted. They crept off the porch and began following me without a sound. They stayed about five feet behind, slinking along in the quiet way that cats do.

Please leave me alone, I thought, but the three cats, like three silent ghosts, kept following. I crossed Mirror Avenue. I passed a row of houses. I cut through Tanner Park. And they stayed with me the whole time, prowling. They didn't hiss or mew or make a single sound. They just followed.

Finally, when I reached the school, they stopped. In one corner of the parking lot, they circled one another a few times, the three-legged cat limping, and they sat down. I kept walking, and the distance between us grew. Soon I was twenty feet away, then forty, and finally, it seemed, they'd let me go.

But they kept watching me. They stayed perched right on the asphalt and fixed their shining eyes on me, even as I crossed the parking lot and ducked through the metal double doors.

I tried not to think about them throughout the day . . . but everything that had happened, with Mom and Licorice and now these three lurking cats, made my skin feel tingly. My face, my back, my legs—all tingly.

In Math class, when Mr. Wilson gave us time to work on

our assignment, I got up to sharpen my pencil and I peeked out the window.

They were still there, in the same corner of the parking lot, lying on their bellies. I know this next part sounds crazy, but when I looked out from Mr. Wilson's classroom, their three heads turned my way all at once. From across the parking lot, one of them—the one with three legs—even stood up.

I stumbled back to my desk.

When the day ended and the bell rang, I started for home. But there weren't just three of them in the parking lot now.

There were six.

They'd been joined by a white cat with only one ear, a gray cat with burrs caught in its fur, and a spotted cat with a limp.

They looked at me. All six of them at once.

I started running.

I bolted past them, and all together they slinked behind me, prowling and weaving past one another.

I ran back through Tanner Park and across Mirror Avenue. I ran over sidewalks and grass and across front yards. And still, they followed—six cats with missing fur and eyes and legs and tails.

At home, I burst through the door and slammed it shut. I peered through the peephole, panting, as the six cats settled onto my front lawn.

I breathed. "It's fine," I said out loud. "It's totally fine." I counted to twenty. I went into the kitchen. Licorice's litter box was still there, tucked into the corner.

I tried to eat a snack, but couldn't.

I felt them on the other side of the door. I knew they were staring at it—maybe even staring through it—waiting for me to come out again.

And I knew why the cats had come. Because of Licorice and the cornfield. But there was something I didn't understand. Sure, Licorice had been my cat, and sure, I had stayed silent when Mom had dumped him by the side of the road. But Mom had been the one who'd done it.

So why were the cats following me?

That night, before switching off my light, I peeled back my curtain and peered outside. They were still there, in the front yard, facing my window.

Only now there were nine of them. One of the new cats had a crooked scar running down its face. All nine looked thin and hungry. All nine were broken in some way.

I remembered what Mom had said when we'd dumped Licorice.

Cats have nine lives.

Nine cats. Nine lives.

And then I remembered what I had said when we'd dumped Licorice.

Nothing.

I walked carefully through the house without waking Mom and creaked open the front door. The night was dark except for the cats' eyes, which glowed yellow. I stepped out into the shadows wearing only my pajama shorts and a long baggy shirt. The air felt cold on my bare legs. I went down the porch steps and onto the damp lawn. The cats' eyes followed me.

"I know why you're here," I said.

The cats didn't move. They kept looking at me, the same way Licorice had as our car drove away.

"Look," I said. "I know it was wrong."

The three-legged cat tilted its head.

"My mom." I pointed to the house. "I should have said something. I should have stopped her."

The orange cat with the missing eye, the one who'd shown up first, sauntered forward. It raised one paw and held it in the air for a few seconds. And then, as if it were some kind of signal, it brought the paw down and scratched the ground three times.

That's when the cats attacked.

They screeched and yowled. All nine of them.

And they came for my legs.

Together, they swirled in a blur of fur and claws, their teeth and eyes flashing.

I ran for the house, trying not to trip on them, but four of the cats leaped onto the porch and blocked the door. They raised their paws and hissed.

The first scratch, just below my left knee, only stung a little.

I bolted for the side of the house, thinking I'd go in the back door, but again, they were too fast. They swarmed and swirled, nine blurs, and they blocked the back, too.

That's when a tiny paw—I'm not sure which cat it belonged to—raked across my right shin, leaving three thin trails of blood.

I burst away from my house, running up the street. I didn't know what else to do. But they came for me, screeching and hissing.

Heading left up Birch Bark Drive and right onto Harrison, I ran as fast as I could. Barefoot, panting. And they followed. My feet slapped the sidewalk, stinging. But I sprinted. If I slowed, claws raked at my calves. It wasn't long before sticky blood trickled down my ankles.

They swarmed. They circled. They turned me this way and that.

My lungs burned. But I ran. My legs ached and pulsed. But I kept going. I would have cried if I'd thought to, but they kept coming and coming and coming.

The smell of my sweat filled the night.

Finally, after what felt like forever, the one-eyed orange cat darted in front of me, turned, and hissed.

I stopped, panting. I'd run down streets and sidewalks, through intersections and neighborhoods, barefoot. The soles of my feet ached and burned. Where was I?

Around me, the other cats stopped, too. Everything fell

quiet. A night breeze blew, and beside me, corn rustled in a field.

And I knew where they'd brought me. It was the spot where we'd dumped Licorice.

I was tired, scratched, and bleeding. The nine cats stood still.

"I'm sorry," I said. "I really am sorry. I should have said something. I should have stood up to her."

The cats hissed as they formed a circle.

I waited for their final attack. I hunched my shoulders and shielded my face with my arms.

The wind picked up, and the corn rustled in the night breeze.

But the cats didn't come.

Instead, the white one stepped into the swishing corn and disappeared. Then the one with half a tail did the same thing. One by one, the cats stepped into the corn. There had been nine of them. But soon there were six, then four, then two. Finally it was just me and the one-eyed orange leader.

I sank down in the dirt by the side of the road. My legs burned with scratches and sweat.

"I'm so sorry," I said. The orange cat paced before me. "Please believe me."

At last the orange cat slunk into the corn and, like the others, disappeared.

I was alone by the side of the road.

Like Licorice.

I put my head between my knees, and tears finally came. My legs were streaked with half-dried blood, but they'd let me go. The cold breeze licked my skin, and I shivered.

Then I heard a rustling in the corn, and two green-yellow eyes appeared in the shadows. A completely black cat—black ears, black legs, black paws—stepped out of the corn.

"Licorice," I said.

He slinked up and nuzzled his head against one of my scratched legs.

"Are you okay?" I said. I wiped tears from my cheeks.

He licked one of my cuts with his sandpapery tongue.

"It's okay," I said. I picked him up and put him in my lap. "We're going to be okay."

I stood, bleeding and tired, holding Licorice in my arms. The moon came out from behind a cloud. In the rustling corn, there were no signs of the nine cats, no glowing eyes peering out. And I knew why the broken cats—the nine lives—had come for me and not for Mom.

I cuddled Licorice. I fondled his velvety ears between my fingers and thumb.

"Let's go home," I said.

And cradling my cat, I began the long walk back.

THE STAIN ON THE CAFETERIA FLOOR

"**Y**OU'RE such a klutz, Janet," said Malia as the dimes she'd been holding clattered to the tile floor. She'd been feeding them to the soda machine in the cafeteria, hoping to buy a Dr. Bubb to go with her lunch, but Janet had just crashed into her, hard, for what must have been the millionth time that year, and sent the dimes scattering.

"Sorry." Janet dropped to the floor and chased after the dimes that were scrambling away like escaped lab rats.

Malia sighed. It wasn't easy having a klutz for a best friend. Just this week, there'd been crashes into lockers, stumbles over garbage cans, and even wild trips on sidewalk cracks.

And now . . . a scattering of dimes on the cafeteria floor.

One dime arced into a corner near the vending machine, and Malia went after it. She tried to stomp on it to stop its rolling. But she missed, and the dime headed toward a moldy-looking stain she'd never noticed before.

Eww, Malia thought. The stain was black with green speckles, like mildew, and it was the shape and size of a peanut, with two bulgy ends. The idea of the dime—her dime—touching that stain made her stomach lurch. But the coin was too far away and moving too fast.

It rolled right onto the stain.

And then something happened that made Malia gasp.

The dime vanished.

Like a popping bubble, one second the dime was there, spinning on the cafeteria tile, and the next second it touched the stain and ... *poof!* ... it was gone.

Malia shivered. "Whoa," she said. "Did you see that?" She moved closer to the stain.

"See what?" Janet gathered the last few scattered coins, stood up, tripped on her untied shoelace, and dropped all the dimes a second time.

Malia shook her head. "One of the dimes," she said. "It just, like, disappeared when it touched ... that." She pointed.

"Are you sure?" Janet said. "Did it maybe roll under the machine?" She crouched and peered under the vending machine.

"No," Malia said. "It rolled onto that." She pointed again.

Janet scrunched her face. "Gross."

Malia took a step toward the stain, but Janet grabbed her by the elbow.

"Don't go near it," she said. "It's nasty."

"Give me a dime," Malia said. Janet picked one up and passed it. Slowly Malia moved into the corner. She knelt and held the dime a few inches over the stain.

"Okay," she said. "Watch."

Malia let go of the dime. It hit the stain and it should have plinked on the floor and spun to a stop. But it didn't. It didn't clink or ping at all. Instead, it fell *into* the moldy stain, like it had been dropped into a hole. Malia peered at the stain. In its very center, the dime spun and grew smaller, going down, down, down.

"No way," Malia said. She listened for a *plink* but heard nothing. "Did you see that?"

Janet didn't answer.

"That must be what happened to the other dime," Malia said, excitement rising in her voice. "It fell into this... thing."

Janet backed away from the corner. She bumped into the vending machine and stumbled. "It's just a hole in the floor," she said, but her voice quivered.

"No." Malia peered closer. "It's not a hole. It's something else, like a puddle. If you look closely, you can see the tile-floor lines beneath it. See?"

"That doesn't make any sense." Janet shook her head. "If we can see the floor beneath it, then how can the dime fall through?"

"I don't know." Malia reached out a finger.

"No!" Janet said. "Don't touch it."

Malia stopped.

"We don't know what it is." Janet backed away even farther, taking tiny awkward steps.

Malia looked from side to side. The other kids in the cafeteria were doing the usual things—eating, talking, paying them no attention.

"Fine," Malia said. "I won't touch it." Still kneeling, she

pulled a stick of gum from her pocket. She dangled it by one end. Its foil wrapper glistened. She lowered the gum slowly, and when it touched the stain, it hissed and fizzled like a can of soda opening. Malia startled and dropped the gum.

Just like the dime, the stick of gum fell somehow past the floor . . . or through the floor, and, just like the dime, the gum twisted, grew smaller, and disappeared.

"It's like a portal," said Malia.

"Can we please just get away from it?" Janet said from behind her. "I don't like it, Malia. Can we just get away?"

Malia turned. Janet's hands were white.

Malia pursed her lips. She wanted to stay by the stain. She wanted to poke it again, to drop in something else—a balled-up piece of paper or a french fry. Maybe she could even lower something into the stain on a string and pull it back out.

But there was Janet. Her face had gone the color of old notebook paper.

"Yeah," Malia said, standing up slowly. She gathered the rest of her dimes. "You're probably right."

She put a hand on Janet's shoulder as they walked back to their table and nudged her to the left to keep her from walking into Adrian Wingham and his tray of spaghetti.

"You're right," Malia said again when they sat down. "We should leave it alone." But as she ate her turkey sandwich, she glanced, again and again, to the corner by the vending machine.

The next day, when lunch started, Malia said, "I'll meet you at the table," and left Janet in the cafeteria line.

She headed straight for the stain.

At the soda machine, she brought her hand to her mouth.

"No way," she whispered. She couldn't believe it. The stain wasn't the size of a peanut anymore. It was bigger now. Much bigger. As big as Malia's head.

She dropped to the floor and crawled close. Not only had the stain changed size, but it had changed shape, too. It had jagged spikes coming out of it from all sides.

"Malia!" Janet's voice hissed from behind her. "Get away from that thing."

Malia turned.

Janet was holding a lunch tray. Her lips were pressed tight. "You said you would leave it alone," she said.

"But it's changed." Malia pointed.

Janet looked, but she didn't move in closer. She shook her head slowly. "That makes it worse," she said.

"It has spiky things." Malia pointed again.

Janet shifted her lunch tray. Her eyes widened.

"And those spikes," Malia said. "They look kind of like teeth . . . or fangs."

"You don't think this is . . ." Janet trailed off.

"A mouth," Malia finished. "It's not a hole or a portal. It's a mouth."

Janet turned and started to walk away, but Malia jumped up and grabbed her arm.

"If this is a mouth," Malia said, turning Janet back, "that means this... thing... is alive."

Janet didn't speak.

"And the dimes and the stick of gum from yesterday," Malia went on. "They didn't fall into a hole. They got eaten." She couldn't believe it. The stain on the cafeteria floor was *alive*.

It was amazing.

No, not just amazing, Malia realized. It was impossible.

"We need to tell someone," Janet finally said.

"No," said Malia. She liked that the spot sat just thirty feet away from dozens of sixth graders, and somehow only she and Janet had found it. It was a secret discovery—their secret discovery. And it could stay that way.

Besides, the stain had grown. It had actually grown. It could eat and change, and maybe it could even breathe and move and feel.

But how could she explain all this to Janet?

"We can't tell anyone," Malia said. "If we tell, they'll get rid of it."

Janet's eyes widened. "That's what we want," she said. "It needs to go."

"No, it doesn't," Malia said.

Janet's body seemed to go slightly limp. Her lunch tray

drooped. Her milk carton slid off and landed on the floor with a *thwack*.

Malia pursed her lips and thought. She had to convince Janet to stay quiet. But Janet kept looking at the stain and sagging.

"Whatever this thing is," Malia said in a low whisper, "it's ours, Janet. It belongs to us."

"It's not ours. It's—"

"It *is* ours," Malia said quickly. "It's ours because..." She thought very hard. It took her a few seconds, but she found what she wanted to say. "It's ours because we found it and we fed it." She nodded and moved close to Janet, close enough to smell the cafeteria meat loaf on her lunch tray. "We fed it two dimes and a stick of gum. And it grew, and that's because of us."

Janet didn't say anything.

Malia pointed at the stain. "This thing is ours, Janet," she said. "We can't have it removed or wiped out. We have to take care of it."

"But we don't know anything about it," Janet whispered. "We don't know what it is. We don't know where it came from. We don't even know if it's safe. If that thing really is a mouth, then where is the rest of it, Malia? Where?"

That was a good point. Where was the rest of the stain? The rest of its body? And where had the dimes and stick of gum gone? A hint of worry, like a slow-rising moon, crept up in Malia's chest.

But she swallowed it down.

"That doesn't matter," Malia said. "It's safe. I can prove it."

Malia reached into her lunch bag and pulled out her turkey sandwich. She knelt, holding her sandwich out. After a second, she let go. The sandwich hit the stain with a *hiss*. Then it tumbled down, down, down.

Malia waited, but nothing happened.

"See," she said. "No problem."

Without answering and without even picking up her dropped milk, Janet walked away. Malia grabbed the milk and followed, barely noticing when Janet bumped into Reggie Perkins on her way to the lunch table.

—◆—

Whoa, Malia thought when she saw the stain the next day. *That thing must have loved my turkey sandwich.*

Because it was no longer the size of Malia's head.

It had grown to the size of a small table, filling the cafeteria corner. Its spikes had become jagged and sharp.

Twenty feet from the stain, Malia put a hand on Janet's shoulder. Other kids had begun to notice the spot, too.

"What's that?" Malia heard Reggie Perkins say.

"Totally weird," said Marissa Clyde.

"I'm not going anywhere near that thing," said Adrian Wingham, and the other kids in the gathering crowd must have agreed because they were standing far back.

Malia pushed past them and walked closer.

"I'm getting a teacher," Janet said. Before Malia could

answer, Janet turned and ran, her feet making hard slaps on the tile floor.

"Janet, no," Malia called. But it was no use. Janet was off, bumping into kids like a pinball in a chute, her clumsy arms flailing.

Malia moved closer to the stain. It wasn't, she realized, a stain anymore. Now it was more of a... Thing. A giant, spiky Thing.

"Gross," said Mikayla Wood back with the gawking kids.

Malia hunched down. She could feel the other kids watching her, wondering.

Sure, this Thing—whatever it was—looked strange. But what had it done wrong? Eaten a few dimes, a stick of gum, and a turkey sandwich? Should they really punish it for that? Get rid of it?

Still, Malia knew that since other kids had now discovered it, there was nothing she could do. Soon Janet would return with Principal Khan or Janitor Jake or somebody, and that would be that. They'd call important people, men in black suits and women in pencil skirts, probably, and they'd close the school and find some way to kill it.

Yes, Malia realized. That was what they would do to the Thing.

They'd kill it.

"I'm sorry," Malia said to it. It was the first time she'd spoken to the Thing. "I think something bad is about to happen." The kids behind her fell quiet.

She scooted closer to the Thing, right to its edge, and she leaned forward. She peered deep into it, wondering whether the sandwich, the stick of gum, and the dimes were still in there somewhere, falling down, down, down.

"It's over here," Janet cried behind her. "It's been growing, and it's got teeth, and Malia's been feeding it. It's getting bigger every day."

"Slow down," someone called, and Malia thought she recognized the voice of Mr. Perez, the Biology teacher.

Then she felt something familiar—a hard bump, a crash against her back—her eternally klutzy best friend banging into her like she had a million times that year. Hunching over the spiky mouth, Malia started to tip forward. She reached back for help. But next to her, Janet stumbled and wobbled at the Thing's edge. Both girls waved their arms in tiny circles. Malia tried to right herself, to get her balance. But it was no use.

She fell.

Next to her, so did Janet.

And they went down, down, down.

WHEN DAUNTE VANISHED, THEY SAID HE MOVED to OHIO

DAUNTE Coleman saw the devil on his walk to school one October morning.

The Father of All Evil was standing there, half a block up the road, red-skinned and surprisingly thin. He was leaning against the street sign at the corner of Gilbert Drive and Chestnut Way, just hanging out, holding his flame-tipped pitchfork.

No way, Daunte thought, a thrill rising in his chest. *The actual devil.*

Daunte had seen a lot of movies about the devil. His favorite was *Send It to the Underworld*, but he also liked *The Devil and Marty McDuffin* and *If Heaven Can't Have You*.

But this was something else. The devil in flesh and blood.

Awesome, Daunte thought.

He smoothed his black T-shirt. He took a few steps closer. Ollie Finker and Jess Whitcomb, the kids he sat with at lunch, were going to freak when they heard. What if Daunte could talk to the actual devil? Could chat for just a few minutes with the Great and Terrible Beast himself? That'd drive Ollie and Jess nuts. He could almost see the looks on their faces when he told them about how he'd asked the devil if Hell really smelled like rotten eggs and how many people exactly were burning in it right then. Simply thinking about it made Daunte's heart beat a little harder.

But up ahead, something about the living, breathing devil wasn't quite right.

At the street sign, the devil cocked his horned head and sighed heavily. He scuffled his forked hooves lazily at the sidewalk, pushing around fallen October leaves. He dangled his pitchfork loosely in one hand.

Daunte walked closer, and the devil picked at his fingernails. Only they weren't fingernails, Daunte realized. They were more like claws...or talons.

I'm gonna do it, Daunte told himself. *I'm gonna march right up to the devil and have a chat.*

He took a few hurried steps. Other kids, he knew, would have acted differently if they'd seen the devil. They would have lost it. Or run away. Or cried. But Daunte wasn't other kids, he told himself. He was Daunte Coleman. He'd known all the words to the heavy metal song "Dark Eyes of the Devil" since he was nine.

And now the King of Flames himself stood before him bathed in foggy morning light. Daunte picked up his pace.

Still, despite all the movies Daunte had seen and all the screaming music he'd listened to, something about the real devil—his sighing, his leaning, his hoof shuffling—seemed...out of place. Wrong, even. Sure, the devil had massive coiling horns and a flaming pitchfork and leathery red skin, just like Daunte had hoped. But instead of looking menacing or horrific or more ominous than death itself, the devil looked, well, tired. And a bit distracted.

And...bored.

Yes, Daunte realized. The devil looked very, very bored.

Up ahead, the devil shifted his weight from one hoof to the other, and Daunte slapped his combat boots hard on the sidewalk as he walked, hoping to get the devil's attention.

The Demon of the Bottomless Pit didn't even look up. He just stayed there, dangling his pitchfork loosely at his side and lazily picking his claws...though they might have been pincers...or hooks.

As he walked closer, Daunte cleared his throat, deep and rough.

Nothing happened.

It was like Daunte didn't even exist, like Satan didn't care at all about the lone sixth grader swaggering up to him.

Daunte's cheeks grew hot. After all the pitchfork drawings he'd made in his notebook margins, he thought he deserved at least a little respect from the Commander of All Beasts.

But the devil must have disagreed because he was still just scuffing his hooves on the sidewalk, pushing fallen leaves this way and that.

Daunte threw back his shoulders. He counted the sidewalk lines between him and the Creature of the Deep—*six, five, four.*

When he was two sidewalk squares away, he spoke.

"Good morning, Mr. Lucifer, sir," he said. Daunte had

never called anyone *sir* before. But the devil, he figured, would like it.

The devil didn't answer. He twirled his pitchfork slowly and chewed lightly on his...whatever those things were on the ends of his hands.

"Good morning, Mr. Lucifer, sir," Daunte tried again, louder.

Finally the devil shifted. His eyes shone black, with no whites in them, and they glistened like wet tar. Daunte couldn't be sure, but it seemed like the devil kind of rolled them.

"Whatever, kid," the devil said.

Daunte flexed his shoulders beneath his black T-shirt.

Everything was wrong. Totally wrong. Daunte'd expected the devil to chant a curse in an ancient language like Latin or Sanskrit. Or to at least let loose an earthquake-inducing roar.

Where, Daunte wondered, *was the Satanic Rage? The Terror of Ultimate Evil? The awesomeness?* Even the devil's voice, which Daunte had thought would be full of raspy, deep growls that echoed with the Doom of Eternities, seemed wrong. He'd thought the devil's voice would shake the ground and set car alarms blaring. But his voice was soft and high-pitched—not rough and demonic—and it was subtly accented, like the devil was from Vermont or Massachusetts or somewhere in New England.

The Ruler of All Demons shooed Daunte along with his

pitchfork and sneered. It was a sneer that said, *Run along, kid. You're bothering me.*

But running along was the last thing on Daunte's mind.

This was his chance—his one chance—to meet the devil. Besides, he'd seen something in the devil's sneer that finally made sense—something that made goose bumps rise on his arms.

The devil's teeth. They were made of fire.

Each tooth was a tiny pointed flame, about the size of a candle flame, and in all the movies Daunte had ever watched, he'd never seen anything like those teeth.

Flaming teeth, Daunte thought. *Now that's what I'm talking about.* The hair on his neck prickled.

"I have questions for you, O Speaker of Darkness, sir," Daunte said.

The devil closed his eyes and breathed out a long, hissing sigh. "You've got to be kidding me," he said. He let his dangling pitchfork swing loosely in his hand. Its flaming tips scraped the sidewalk and made dark scorch marks on the concrete that hissed and smoked.

Daunte leaned in as the scorch marks sizzled and died.

"That's more like it," he said quietly. Above him, the devil shook his head, and one of his coiled horns clinked against the street sign's metal pole. Daunte pointed at the sidewalk. "I behold your awesomeness, sir."

"Oh, stop it," the devil said. "Stop it with all the 'awesome' and 'sir' stuff, kid."

"But—" Daunte said, and he didn't know how to continue. This wasn't going the way he'd hoped.

"Look, kid," the devil said without looking at Daunte directly. "Believe it or not, I haven't made the trip all the way from Hell today just to visit some pesky kid. I'm a pretty busy guy with an important job, okay? Can you understand that?" His voice rose, and his flaming teeth seemed to grow and stretch higher. He waggled his pitchfork in front of Daunte's face. "I've got a big day ahead, and all I want out of the next five minutes is a bit of a break, all right? So it's time for you to head to school and leave me in peace."

With that, the devil stomped one hoof, and the school bell in the distance rang. Daunte was sure there were at least ten minutes left before school started, but there the bell was, ringing out over houses and trees.

"You made the school bell ring!" Daunte exclaimed, realizing he'd witnessed a moment of the devil's power. "That was—" He was going to say *awesome*, but he stopped himself.

"It means you're late," the devil said, "so…" The devil pointed his pitchfork at the brown school building down the street.

But Daunte wasn't ready to leave. Not yet. Not until more things started going like they were supposed to—like the flaming teeth and the early ringing bell. So Daunte folded his arms and planted his feet.

"Oh, come on," the devil said, and his teeth flared. "Kid, what's it going to take? How do I get rid of you?"

Daunte thought. There had to be something he could do to get the devil to act more . . . well . . . devilish.

"Three questions," Daunte said. "Answer three of my questions, and I'll leave." Daunte wasn't sure what he wanted to ask the devil, exactly, but with three questions he was sure he could pry out a few awesomely dark details.

The devil's thin, pointed tail swished from side to side. He sighed. He twirled his pitchfork slowly, almost hypnotically. Daunte followed the flaming tips round and round.

"Fine," the devil said. "Three questions. Then you beat it."

Daunte couldn't believe it. He'd been granted three questions—three questions to ask the Great Destroyer (who admittedly wasn't exactly what Daunte'd expected, but still). Daunte pressed his lips together and rubbed his hands. He wanted to get his questions just right. He wanted them to reveal dark secrets.

"Question number one," Daunte said.

Daunte stopped. He had a thought.

Could he trust the devil to answer his questions honestly? After all, he was dealing with the Father of Lies and Deception.

I'll just have to hope, he told himself. He went on.

"What's Hell like?" Daunte said, settling on his first question.

Daunte imagined Hell sometimes. He even tried to draw pictures of it occasionally, with boiling pools of oil everywhere and sizzling walkways.

"Hell is…" the devil said, and Daunte leaned close for the answer. He smelled a hint of burning hair coming off the devil. "…unpleasant."

The devil stopped.

"What else?" Daunte said.

The devil shook his head. "That was my answer. Next question."

"No way," Daunte said. "You've got to tell me more than that. Is the real Hell like the Hell in *Netherworld Lost*, with lots of chains and steam? Or is it more like the Hell in *Swelling Inferno*, different for each person?"

"Are those your second and third questions?" the devil said.

"No!" Daunte blurted. "Don't answer those."

The devil gave a fiery smile. He was not making this easy.

For a few seconds, Daunte said nothing. He hooked his thumbs through his backpack straps and shifted it, feeling the weight of his stuff inside—the Algebra book he hadn't opened in weeks, the Geography binder he also hadn't touched in quite a while, and, in the bottom of his backpack, a pile of wrappers from candy bars he'd stolen from a group of fifth graders.

The flaming points of the devil's pitchfork seemed to rise, and the devil spun the pitchfork a few times, casually.

"Let's go," the devil said. "I haven't got all day."

Daunte blinked hard and focused on the leathery skin

of the devil's hairless chest and how it seemed to glow even in the quiet morning light, and on the curve of the razored horns on top of the devil's head, and also on the flaming teeth—*especially* the flaming teeth. Sure, the devil wasn't everything Daunte had hoped for, but still, the flaming teeth were something.

As if he'd read Daunte's mind, the devil opened his mouth wider and his teeth flamed higher. The tiny fires stretched, and a wave of heat washed over Daunte.

Did the flaming teeth burn the devil's mouth, Daunte wondered. *Did they cause him eternal agony?* Now that would be truly awesome—eternal burning you could never escape. Awesome.

The devil flared his teeth once more, then snapped his mouth shut. "Is that what you wanted to see, kid?" the devil said. "Are you satisfied now? Will you move along?"

He brought his pitchfork down. He swung it like the pendulum of a clock and gestured with it at the school in the distance.

"You owe me two more questions," Daunte said, not giving up. "So here's question number two." He wanted to see the devil's teeth again, wanted to watch them flare and wave. "Your teeth...do they..."

But Daunte didn't know how to finish.

"Do they burn?" the devil said, leaning down slightly. "Do they hurt?"

Daunte nodded.

"Nah," the devil said. "They don't hurt, kid."

Daunte was slightly disappointed.

The devil scuffed the sidewalk with one hoof. "They used to," he said, "but they don't anymore. Once, they blistered my tongue and boiled my spit. But you get used to things, Daunte. Even in Hell. Next question."

Daunte touched his own mouth and imagined a fire inside. And that's when he realized something. The devil had called him by his name—not *kid*, but *Daunte*. The devil started picking his talons again.

"You know my name?" Daunte said.

The devil looked directly at him. For the first time, he looked Daunte in the eyes. It sent a chill down his neck.

"Of course I know your name," the devil said slowly. "I know everything about you, Daunte Frederick Coleman. Everything."

The devil swung his pitchfork back and forth like a hypnotist's watch.

The Firstborn of Sin said my name, Daunte thought, and for a second this made him proud. His heart pounded. Ollie and Jess would never believe it. Never.

But then something changed. Daunte felt an uneasy itching swell up in his throat. This new feeling scratched and burned, just a little, and it seemed to come from Daunte's stomach.

The feeling had something to do with the devil saying his name—his full name—out loud.

The devil smiled, baring his flaming teeth.

This new feeling wasn't...awesome.

Daunte shook himself. *Stay focused*, he told himself. *Keep it together.*

He couldn't get distracted. He was with the devil. The actual devil. And he had one question left, one question before he'd have to leave the devil behind, so it needed to be a good one. It needed to be perfect. Daunte blinked hard, and he swallowed the new scratchy feeling down.

In front of him, the devil twirled his pitchfork. He swished it slowly back and forth. Its flaming tips smoked, and the devil let the smoke trickle up to Daunte's face.

The smoke smelled old...ancient. And it gave Daunte an idea.

"Question number three," Daunte said slowly. He felt a little dizzy, maybe from the smoke, but he pointed at the devil's pitchfork. "Can I hold that? For just a second?"

Now that would be truly awesome, Daunte told himself. *Wouldn't it? Touching the pitchfork of the Monster of All Horrors?*

The devil straightened but didn't answer.

Yes, Daunte thought. *That would be totally, completely, endlessly awesome.*

"So?" Daunte said. "Will you let me?"

The devil looked at Daunte and let out a small, quiet laugh.

"You've got nerve, kid," the devil said. "Did anyone ever tell you that? You've got a lot of nerve."

Daunte extended a hand. He opened his palm and waited. The uneasy feeling—the scratchy heat—boiled in his throat a second time. That feeling, Daunte knew, had something to do with what the devil had said before. *I know your name. I know everything about you, Daunte Frederick Coleman. Everything.* The devil extended the pitchfork. It was just three inches from Daunte's open hand, and the scratchy feeling spread from Daunte's throat to his whole body.

Daunte froze.

Something was wrong. Maybe it had been wrong this whole time.

Something wasn't adding up. Daunte was certain of it. It had something to do with the devil knowing his name. But it was more than that. It was the devil waving his pitchfork around, looking eternally bored, flashing his flaming teeth, leaning against the street sign's pole . . . It was the devil showing up on Gilbert Drive in the first place.

What was the Deceiver of Innocents doing here?

Why had he come?

And then it hit Daunte.

This was the devil. *The actual devil.*

Daunte had seen the movies. He'd listened to the songs. The devil always had a plan. Always. He didn't do things for no reason. And he never got bored.

Daunte moved to pull his hand back, to get it away from the devil, but it was too late. The devil moved like a thunderclap and slapped the pitchfork into Daunte's open palm.

Daunte gasped, feeling the hot steel in his hand.

"Oh, Daunte Frederick Coleman," the devil said. "Remember that you asked for this. You asked for all of this, kid."

Daunte's eyes widened. He opened his mouth to speak, but the words wouldn't come out.

Something was happening. In his mouth.

There was heat on his gums and tongue. Bad heat. It was like that time he'd eaten a ghost pepper on a dare. He coughed and blew out short puffs of air, his lips forming a tight O.

It didn't help. The burning on his tongue and gums grew worse. The devil started to laugh—high and quiet.

Daunte fanned a hand in front of his mouth.

Still, the heat rose, and it wasn't just heat now. It was pain. Daunte jumped up and down. He beat at his mouth with his hands. It felt like he was holding hot coals in his cheeks.

What's happening? he tried to ask the devil, but the sounds that came out were nothing like words.

He fell to his knees. He rolled from side to side, and the devil's laugh swelled. The insides of Daunte's lips and cheeks began to char and bleed. His tongue blistered.

The pitchfork, he realized. *This has something to do with the pitchfork.* He needed to get rid of it. He tried to throw it away.

He flailed. But the pitchfork stayed in his hand. He tried to fling it, to pry it out of his palm, but it was stuck, as if welded permanently to his skin.

A hissing, popping sound filled the air. In his mouth, Daunte's spit began to boil.

And he knew.

His teeth had turned... to flames.

To tiny, pointed flames.

He curled up and writhed.

He closed his eyes. He tried to stand but couldn't. Above him, the laughing devil spoke.

"I wouldn't feel too bad about this, kid," he said. Daunte forced himself to look up. Where the devil had stood before, there was now a small old man in a gray suit. He had deeply creased cheeks and gray hair, and even through the searing pain in his mouth, Daunte heard something familiar in the man's high voice and his New England accent. "I made the same mistake myself, more years ago than I can count."

Daunte gagged.

"And I really do remember how this feels," the old man said calmly. Daunte tried to scream for help but couldn't. "What I said before is true, kid. You do get used to it. And someday, if you're lucky, maybe you'll track down someone who'll take it all away from you—just like you took it from me."

The gray man winked. Daunte reached out a hand, but the old man turned and walked away, and black, tarry tears welled up in Daunte's eyes.

Daunte's skin seemed to be hardening, turning to thick leather. Every second, he found it harder to breathe, harder to move, harder to think. A tearing pain spiked on either side of his head, and sharp horns pierced through his skin and grew and curled.

Half a block up, the gray man turned and smiled a bright smile full of, not flames, but teeth. Finally the old devil walked on, leaving Daunte to writhe and squirm, to adjust to a life of burning and flame, and to learn to walk on hooves.

Daunte screamed then, primal and long.

The scream echoed with the Doom of Eternities.

The Color of Ivy✦

IVY found the marker under her desk.

She'd felt something with her foot while Mr. Jameson had been reviewing that day's homework assignment—a long worksheet on prepositions—so she'd peered down to check what was there.

The marker was thin and glittery and greenish black, and she'd never seen anything quite like it. She bent and picked it up.

It was warm, as if it had been out in the sun. She removed the cap, and its dark tip glistened. Bringing it to her nose, she smelled its ink. It was sweet, like honey.

I wish this were mine, Ivy thought. If it were, she knew exactly what she'd draw—a dark, enchanted forest, with lots of hanging vines. It was the perfect color.

She considered stuffing the marker into her backpack quietly. Instead, she tapped Kiara's shoulder in front of her.

"Is this yours?" she whispered, holding up the marker. "Did you drop it?"

Kiara shook her head and went back to the prepositions worksheet. Ivy waved the marker slightly, showing it to the other students sitting around her. Each one shrugged. "Not mine," said Malcolm. *No*, mouthed Kirk. Ivy set the marker on her notebook. It must have been dropped by a student from an earlier class. It looked new and fancy and was probably part of a set. Ivy imagined it lined up neatly in a plastic case with other glittering colors.

She squinted at a sign that hung in the front of every classroom, beside the clock.

PLEASE RETURN ALL LOST OR STOLEN ITEMS TO THE MAIN OFFICE.

She fingered the marker and rolled it back and forth on her notebook. Its color was like moss on an old brick wall. Ivy liked that. She picked it up and drummed it on the edge of her desk.

It really is the perfect color, she thought.

It was the color of ivy, she realized—her color.

The color of Ivy.

She smiled.

She popped the cap off and flattened her left hand on her prepositions worksheet, spreading her fingers. Since the marker was, after all, her color, she decided to try it out on her own skin.

I did look for the owner, she thought. *Besides, it's just a marker.*

Still, the marker's glittery color and perfumed scent told her the marker was different. Special.

On the back of her hand, she drew a strand of ivy. She started by making a curving, twisting vine just under her knuckles. The ink came out warm, the exact same glittery greenish black as the marker's cap.

She drew three leaves on her strand of ivy—one leaf for each letter in her name. One for the *I*, one for the *V*, and one for the *Y*. When she had finished, she blew on her hand softly. She touched the vine with a finger, testing to see if the ink would smudge. It didn't. Then she twisted her hand under the classroom lights and let the greenish glittery ink shimmer.

She had never been much of an artist, but Ivy had to admit it: the strand of ivy on her hand looked good—almost real.

It was nearly perfect—this thing she was named for on her skin in the best color ever.

Just then, the bell rang, jarring Ivy back to class.

"Before you leave," Mr. Jameson called out over the noise of students gathering folders and stuffing backpacks, "make sure your names are on your prepositions worksheets, and turn them in at the basket."

Ivy peered down at her homework. She'd forgotten to fill in the blank space at the top of her page for her name.

She gripped the marker. Then she had an idea.

Instead of filling in her name, she could draw a strand of ivy with her perfect new marker. Mr. Jameson would see the twisting vine on the line where her name usually went, and he'd figure out whose assignment it was, wouldn't he?

She decided to go for it. She started with the twisting stalk and then added three leaves. One for the *I*, one for the *V*, and one for the *Y*. Again, her vine—her "name-vine," she decided to call it—looked perfect. Almost real. The greenish-black ink glittered.

She stood and dropped her assignment in the basket. By the time she got back to her desk, most of the other students had filed out of the classroom.

Peering around, she zipped the marker into the front pocket of her backpack, which she slung quickly over one shoulder.

— ~ —

When she got home, she plopped her backpack onto her unmade bed and pulled out the marker. She wanted to label her stuff—to write her name-vine on lots of things.

She started by scrawling across the top of her journal. The journal's cover was light orange, and the name-vine looked perfect stretching across the top. Then she pulled out her school notebooks and binders and labeled them with her name-vine, too. She drew the vine on the softballs in her closet and on her bat, and she even doodled it on the small tags of her stuffed animals.

Where else can I put it? she thought.

She knew some people wrote their names on the inside covers of their books in case they ever got lost or borrowed, so she went to her bookshelf and started sliding books out. Inside the cover of each one, she drew her twisting vine.

As she drew the leaves, she mouthed the letters of her name. *I-V-Y.*

It took her nearly half an hour to label everything in her room, and when she finished, she zipped the marker back into the front pocket of her backpack. She looked once more at the name-vine on her hand. She made a fist, twisted it, and the drawing, complete with four leaves, seemed to ripple.

Four leaves? she thought. She counted them again.

Yes, there were definitely four—one leaf under each of her four knuckles.

She was certain she'd drawn just three leaves when she'd found the marker—one leaf for her *I*, one leaf for her *V*, and one leaf for her *Y*. Since then she'd drawn the same thing maybe fifty times.

There had been three leaves. Just three. Each time.

She pulled a book from her shelf and opened it. There, on the inside of the front cover, was a four-leafed vine.

She checked the cover of her journal. Four leaves. She checked her school notebooks and binders and her softballs and her bat. She checked the tags on her stuffed animals.

They all had four leaves.

I messed up, Ivy thought. *I got distracted, and I drew an extra leaf.*

But how could she have made that same mistake over and over?

She shook her hand and flexed her fingers, and the vine below her knuckles seemed to twist and stretch.

The next morning, she showered, but she tried to keep her left hand out of the streaming water. Even though she'd messed up her name-vine by adding an extra leaf, she still liked it and wanted to keep it from washing off. So she held her left hand toward the back of the shower and soaped and shampooed with her right. Still, the vine got a little wet from steam and splashes.

Stepping out of the shower, Ivy slipped into her bathrobe and dabbed her hand lightly with a towel, careful not to wipe or smear.

She lifted the towel and gasped.

The inky vine now curled down her hand and around her wrist. It had more leaves. Lots more leaves—Ivy counted quickly—nine of them in all. Most were small, as if they'd just sprouted.

She ran to her room and pulled her journal from her desk drawer.

The vine across the top now twisted and sprawled down the journal's cover. It had nine leaves. She checked her binders and books. Nine leaves. She checked her stuffed animal tags, her softballs, and her bat.

The vines all had nine leaves.

She looked back to the vine on her hand.

The water from the shower, she thought. *I watered the ivy and it grew.*

And the other vines had, too. Whatever happened to

the vine on her hand, it seemed, happened to the rest of them.

What if they keep growing? she thought. She started breathing quickly. *What if the vine on her hand spread up her arm and onto her face?*

What if it covered her whole body?

How would she look with glittery vines covering her from head to toe, spiraling around her eyes, wrapping around her neck?

She brought a hand to her throat.

The color of Ivy, she thought.

Suddenly her name-vine didn't seem so cool. Ivy's heart thudded. She had to get rid of it. Whatever this thing was, it was spreading. She wanted it gone.

She bolted back to the bathroom, turned on the tap, and grabbed a bar of soap, but before she plunged her hand under the water, she stopped.

Would the vine even wash off?

She turned the faucet down to a trickle and let a few drops drip onto her hand. The ivy glittered, and then the vine twined and grew, sprouting leaves and circling a few inches higher up her arm.

No, she thought. She grabbed a dry washcloth and scrubbed till her skin hurt, but the vine kept growing. It swirled to her elbow. It sprouted more leaves.

She grabbed her hair dryer and blasted it on high. She pointed it at the vine and held it steady. Her skin turned red and burned. But it didn't help. The vine may have changed color slightly, taking on the faintest hint of brown. But it was still there, shiny and glittering.

She ran to her room. The vines were everywhere. They circled her softballs and spiraled around her bat. They covered her journal and bled out from the inside covers of her books. They wrapped around her stuffed animals' legs and arms and stomachs.

What is this? she thought. *What have I done?*

~•~

She wore a long-sleeved sweater to school that day, and when no one was looking, she pushed up the sleeve and checked the vine. It hadn't grown any more, but it hadn't shrunk or shriveled either. It just stayed there, twisted around her arm.

All day, she avoided water.

When she used the bathroom after second-period Math, she left without washing her hands. And during lunch, when it started raining, her friends Madison and Carrie ran outside to splash, but she moved away from the doors, deeper into the safety of the dry school. And whenever she was thirsty, she filled her water bottle, one-handed, in one of the school's drinking fountains, careful not to splash, and she sipped the water through a tall, thin straw. Just in case.

In English, Mr. Jameson held up her prepositions worksheet from the day before.

"Someone," he said, "forgot to put their name on this."

The margins of the worksheet were completely covered in greenish-black vines. "But that same someone did take the time to draw a jungle."

Ivy didn't speak.

"No one's claiming it?" Mr. Jameson said. Ivy pulled her sweater down over her knuckles, far enough to cover the vine on her hand.

"Very well," Mr. Jameson said. "Someone will be getting a zero."

She didn't sleep well that night, not with all the vines in her room. It was like she was camping in a rain forest. The next morning, she sat on the edge of the bathtub, studying the vine on her arm. It had lost some of its glitter. She was sure of it. A few leaves even seemed to be drooping, and she thought that maybe the occasional crease and crinkle were showing up in the twisting stalk.

The vine hadn't yet reached her shoulder. Even better, it hadn't grown at all since she'd kept away from water. Neither had any of the other vines in her room. She wasn't sure, but the vines, she thought, were starting to look a little thirsty.

She backed away from the bathtub. Instead of washing and drying and curling her hair, she pulled her hair back into a simple ponytail.

After breakfast, she checked the weather forecast. No rain, so she headed to school.

That night, her mother leaned in close, squinted at her hair, and said, "Ivy, did you remember to use shampoo today?"

Ivy shrugged.

"Your hair looks a little greasy."

Ivy shrugged again.

"Well, don't forget tomorrow."

Ivy ran her vine-free hand through her hair. Her fingers picked up the slightest oily film.

But the vines are shriveling, she thought. She was sure of it. They weren't a deep greenish black anymore. They were a greenish brown. And they hardly glittered at all. When she checked the vine on her arm before going to bed, two of the leaves had even fallen off—one on her forearm and one by her wrist. If Ivy could just keep her arm dry for a few more days, she was sure the vines—all of them—would vanish.

The next morning, Ivy locked the bathroom door. She grabbed a dry towel and wrapped it around her arm. Then she turned on the water.

She didn't even take off her clothes. The water ran while she sat against the wall, on the far side of the room.

She let the water run for ten minutes, long enough for her mother to hear and the mirror to start fogging. Then, with her arm still in the towel and stretched out far behind her, she cranked the water off.

Before leaving the bathroom, she put on extra deodorant. In her bedroom, she checked the vine on her journal. No more leaves had dropped, but its stalk was definitely thinning. Definitely.

Ivy tucked her hair up into a purple baseball cap, and she managed to leave the house without coming face-to-face with her mother.

⌐ ⌐

The vines proved harder to kill than Ivy had hoped. Five days later, they still had four leaves. On her arm, the leaves were in a clump halfway between her wrist and elbow. The stalk on her hand, though, was definitely brown.

Ivy kept her hair tucked up in a bun now. It had become stringy and oily, and it stuck together in greasy clumps. And though she'd never had acne, families of zits had popped up on her face and neck.

But she felt so close—so close to killing the vines and being free.

Still, she knew her mother could ruin everything. All it would take was for her to get one close look at Ivy's hair or to inhale one big whiff of Ivy's moldering smell, and her mother would order her into a big tub of warm water and soap.

So Ivy became "too busy" to spend much time at home. She told her mother she needed to attend study groups at the library. She needed to stay after school and complete extra credit. She needed to meet a tutor at the park. When she did have to be at home, Ivy wore long sleeves and hoodies that hid her face and hair, and she ate her meals quickly. If her mother tried to talk to her, she muttered about homework

and darted off to her room, where she sat surrounded by the slowly withering vines.

She just needed to hang on, she told herself. Just a little longer. She could handle the bits of grime around her toenails. She could deal with the black grit behind her ears. She could even accept that no amount of deodorant could cover her smell anymore—a smell that was something like a head of lettuce rotting away in an old locker room.

Because when she thought of what might happen if she took a bath—how the vines would stretch across her whole body, wrapping around her ankles, tracing along the grooves in her ears—she refused to quit.

Not now.

Over the next three days, only one more leaf dropped. But the vines on her arm and her journal and her books and her stuffed animals seemed to be getting thinner.

She felt gritty all the time, and in class the kids who sat next to her scooted their desks as far from her as they could.

One day at lunch, she sat in her usual place and waited for Madison and Carrie to join her. She chewed her sloppy joe. She looked around.

Then she heard whispers.

You can smell her from here! She's like a garbage dump!

You can actually see the grease in her hair!

We should call her Poison Ivy!

Halfway through her sloppy joe, she scanned the

lunchroom and found Madison and Carrie. They were eating together and laughing at another table far away.

It will be okay, she told herself. In a few more days, the vines would be dead. If she could just hang on, then soon—very soon—she could fix this. She would clean herself up and get back to a normal life.

— —

Five days later, the vines still weren't gone. She didn't understand it. All the leaves had vanished, but the brown stalks remained.

Her hands, she decided, were the dirtiest part of her. She'd spilled a glob of grape jelly on them the day before, and she'd tried wiping it off with a dry napkin, but it just smeared the jelly into her layer of existing grime. When she balled her fingers into a fist, they stuck together as she tried to open them.

At dinner, her mother sniffed the air, peered at her eyes, and asked Ivy to peel back her hoodie.

"I have a ton of homework," Ivy said, standing up and pushing away her plate.

But her mother said, "Stop, honey! The hoodie. Now." And then she said, "I haven't seen your face in weeks."

Slowly, Ivy lifted her hands and pushed back her hood. She kept her head down.

Her mother gasped.

"Ivy," her mother said, standing up. "Oh, Ivy. What is this?"

Ivy folded her arms and pressed her lips. How could she possibly explain?

"Why are you doing this to yourself?" Her mother reached out and felt Ivy's hair. "You're covered in ... grime," she said. "You're going to get sick."

Ivy shook her head.

"You need a shower," her mother said, her voice rising. "Right now. How long has it been?"

Ivy shrugged.

"You have to take care of yourself."

Ivy didn't speak. She turned away and lifted her sleeve. The vine was still there on her arm. It was faint, barely a thin brown line, but she could see it trailing down her skin like a winding vein.

She shook her head.

"Honey, this isn't a request!" her mother said.

But without a word, Ivy walked to her room, closed her door, and locked it.

A few minutes later, her mother knocked. "You'll shower, young lady, and you'll wash your hair, or you'll be grounded for a month."

"A month?" Ivy said quietly, checking the vines around her. They were so thin. So brown. "I'll take it."

In school, hallway crowds parted around her. Kids who sat next to her plugged their noses. Girls left the bathroom quickly when she walked in.

The creases in her knuckles became crusted with dirt. The grooves at the bases of her fingernails became caked with black gunk. The crannies inside her ears grew crusty and hard. The backs of her knees turned grubby. No one talked to her.

She sat alone. She studied alone. She ate alone.

She spent even less time at home. She sat in the library. She wandered around parks. She hid behind trees in her own backyard.

Almost there, she told herself as she entered her room one night and had to squint to see the disappearing vines. *Just a little more.*

On Ivy's twenty-third day without a shower, Mr. Jameson passed out a worksheet on adverbs. When he handed one to Ivy, he shook his head slightly as he looked down at her. Her hair, which had once been soft and wavy, was now thick and clumpy.

Ivy reached for her worksheet, and her fingers left small grease smudges on the paper. At the top of her assignment, a line asked for her name. Ivy reached into her backpack for a pencil, and she pulled out, instead, the marker.

Somehow, she'd managed to forget about it. She'd been so focused on the vines, so focused on killing them, that she hadn't even touched it.

But it had been there, this whole time, in her backpack.

She set the marker on her desk and she pulled up her sleeve to check the vine for what must have been the thousandth time. Her skin was flaking. Dirt crusted her arm.

Ivy leaned close and stared. She blinked.

She couldn't believe it.

The vine was gone.

Yes, the vine was gone. It was completely, wonderfully gone.

She checked all her notebooks and binders, pulling them out of her backpack one by one.

There was nothing on them, not even faint lines.

On her arm there was just skin—her greasy, dirt-stained skin.

She closed her eyes and let out a heavy breath.

It's over, she thought. She fought back tears. She thought of her shower at home, how she couldn't wait to turn the knobs and stand beneath the water and let it run off her in murky streams. She would stand there for hours. She would make up for the last twenty-three days. Even if the hot water ran out, she would shampoo her hair over and over. She would scrub her skin with a hard brush, and she would use up a complete bar of soap. No, two. And then she would use body wash—all she could find—and an anti-acne face scrub and globs and globs of conditioner. And when the last crusts of dirt had peeled off and floated down the drain, when she was finally clean, she would dress in newly washed clothes and hug her mother and say she was sorry—she was so, so sorry—and she'd let her mother hold her and breathe in her soapy, perfumey scent for hours.

And then things could become normal again. Maybe the

whispers that surrounded her would stop. And the jokes. And the nose-pluggings.

And maybe, in time, even Madison and Carrie would come back to her.

She took one last look at the greenish-black marker that had started everything, and she bent and set it on the floor beneath her desk. She pushed it away with her foot. Then she reached back into her bag, fumbled for a pencil, and in the space on the adverb worksheet that called for her name, she wrote three clear, block letters.

I-V-Y.

NEAT-O BURRITO

SO I'm walking home from school, strolling down the sidewalk along Magnolia Avenue, and I'm thinking about Caroline Spencer and her green eyes and the way she tucks her hair behind her ears when she makes comments in History class. Lately, I've been thinking a lot about Caroline Spencer and her green eyes and the way she tucks her hair behind her ears when she makes comments in History class, and the truth is, I'm starting to get a little weirded out. I'm ready to get back to thinking about the Red Sox and the hot dogs at Fenway Park and the catcher's mitt I got for my birthday.

But I can't.

Because did I mention that Caroline Spencer has green eyes? Did you know that she tucks her hair behind her ears when she makes comments in History class?

So yeah. I'm walking and kicking at sidewalk pebbles as I go, and I'm telling myself to think about baseball, baseball, baseball.

But it's no use.

Because I'm also thinking about the last two words I said to Caroline Spencer—the last two idiotic words.

Here's what they were:

Neat-o burrito.

No kidding. I actually said those words to her. To Caroline Spencer.

I don't think I've ever said the words *neat-o burrito* to anybody in my entire life. But now they're playing in my mind like they're on a loop or something.

Neat-o burrito. Neat-o burrito. Neat-o burrito.

I'm such an idiot.

Here's what happened:

When the last bell rang at school, I stood up and shouldered my backpack.

And next to me, Caroline Spencer stood up, too.

She tucked her hair, like she does, and I thought for the hundredth time how she walks home in the same direction I walk home—we live on the same street—and so I thought that maybe I'd ask her if she wanted to walk home together.

"Hey, Caroline," I said, and she turned. "Are you walking home now?"

She didn't answer right off. Or maybe she did, and it just felt like forever while I waited to hear what she'd say.

After about two hours, she finally said, "I'd like to, but I can't. It's Tuesday."

I made a face to show I didn't understand.

"On Tuesdays, I stay after to help Miss Sutherland clean the erasers," she said.

I didn't know what to say next, so we both just stood there for a second, looking at each other. My tongue seemed to swell, and I think I might have even started sweating a little. I swallowed hard, and then I said the words. The two idiotic words.

"Neat-o burrito."

Of course Caroline kind of looked at me funny. I mean, why wouldn't she? We both stood there for what felt like another hour, and then she said, "Bye, Matt," sounding a little sad. She turned and walked to the front of the classroom, where she started gathering up the erasers.

Neat-o burrito?

Idiot.

Now, kicking sidewalk pebbles on Magnolia Avenue, I realize what I should have said instead. When Caroline Spencer said she was going to stay after school and clean the erasers, I should have said this:

Wow, you clean the erasers for Miss Sutherland? That's cool. I'll wait for you. That way you won't have to walk home alone.

I nod my head. Yep. That's what I should have said. Idiot.

I find another pebble and send it skittering down the sidewalk and into some bushes.

Or, I realize, I should have said this:

I'll stay after and help you.

Yeah. That's what I should have said. It would have been perfect. I should have offered to help her. I should have been generous, thoughtful, chivalrous. Yes, that's the word. That's what I should have been.

Chivalrous.

But nope.

"Neat-o burrito," I mutter out loud. I shake my head a little. Where did those words even come from?

I come upon a big pebble. It's the size of a quarter, and I kick it as hard as I can.

It bounces down the sidewalk and drops into the gutter. Then it plinks against something metal, something that makes a shiny *thunk* sound. I look, and a gold reflection in the gutter catches my eye. I walk over, and can you believe it? It's a lamp, right there in the gutter.

But it's not the kind of lamp you'd have in your house. It's the kind of lamp you'd rub to make a genie come whooshing out. It's scratched and copper colored, and it's about the size of a football.

"Cool," I say to no one—certainly not to Caroline Spencer, who I guess is still out pounding erasers and won't be coming this way for at least ten more minutes.

Baseball, I tell myself. *Think about baseball.*

Then I pick up the lamp.

I grab it by the little handle thing. It's warm, and there's a long snake carved around the base. I start rubbing it with one hand 'cause that's what you do with a lamp like this, right? I mean, who wouldn't? Of course I know nothing's going to happen. This lamp is just junk someone dumped in the gutter. But no one's around, and it's pretty tempting, so I mutter to myself as I rub the lamp—for fun.

"Oh, great genie of the lamp," I say. "I call you forth."

Then—get this—the lamp starts smoking. Seriously.

It looks like it's gushing steam, like a teapot with a narrow spout puffing away. I startle and drop the lamp, and it clatters back to the gutter.

Then—*Hiss! Boom! Poof!*—there's a genie floating in the air. Just like that. An actual genie. He's got a purple headwrap and a matching little vest and a goatee.

"Who summons me from my slumber?" he says. His voice is deep, and it echoes down Magnolia Avenue. There are a few kids walking on the next block, but they don't turn my way, so I figure they must not be able to see or hear the genie. I guess only I can do that.

Crazy, right?

My mouth drops and I make what my mom calls my "no-way face." But I blink hard, and sure enough, this is all real. There's a genuine genie right there, hovering just over a fire hydrant on Magnolia Avenue.

The genie glares at me. His bottom half funnels down into the lamp, and I can't tell whether he has legs or not.

I snap out of my little trance, and I realize the genie asked me a question, so I say, "Oh, I guess I, um, summoned you."

He looks at me from bottom to top, peering from my shoes to my knees to my chest and finally to my eyes. He licks his lips.

"I'm Matt," I say. I raise one hand and give a little wave. Right after, I wish I hadn't.

The genie sort of drifts around, like a balloon on a string.

"One wish," he says, and then his eyes begin to narrow.

He holds up one finger. All his fingers, even his thumbs, have rings on them. "I will grant you one wish. No more. Then I will return to my slumber."

I thought I got three wishes, not one. Isn't that always the deal? But I'm too amazed to say anything, so I shake myself and try to stick with what's happening.

"Speak your deepest desire." The genie opens his arms. "Speak it, Matt, and I will make your dreams come true."

Your deepest desire. Your dreams come true. The words echo around in my head and I think about—surprise, surprise—Caroline Spencer.

But then I slap myself on the inside.

See, I might be an idiot, but I'm no dummy.

I've read the books. I've seen the movies. I know how this works.

Wishes *never* go the way you plan them. Never. Here's what I mean:

Suppose I ask this genie for a bajillion dollars. What'll probably happen is this. I'll make my wish and hold out my hands ready for money to plop down from the sky. But then, as I'm standing there, looking up, some guy with a clipboard and an official-sounding name—a name like Montgomery Macalister—will stroll up and tell me my parents were just killed in a tragic car accident. He'll tell me my parents owned a huge life insurance policy, and now I'm rich.

Presto! My wish has been granted! And I'll spend the rest of my life orphaned and lonely.

Or say I wish to become the world's best baseball player.

Just like that I'll be smashing home runs on final pitches, and everyone will be begging for my autograph. I'll have my own personal assistant and agent and publicist, and then one day I'll wake up in some fancy bed and realize that I'm a complete fraud. I'll know, deep down, that every other baseball player on earth earned their success through practice and hard work. But not me. I wished my way into it.

I'll spend the rest of my life feeling like a lazy cheater. I don't think I'd like that. I really don't.

That's how wishes work. It's called irony. Or comic justice. Or something.

Well, no thank you!

So yeah, there's this genie—an actual poofy-pantsed genie floating right in front of me—and sure, there's Caroline Spencer—the green-eyed, hair-tucking Caroline Spencer in the back (okay, front) of my mind—but I think for a minute and look at the genie. He's got a devilish grin I didn't notice before. He's also got these hungry-looking eyes. He slithers around in the air, and he wets his lips, waiting, so I say, "No thanks. No wish for me."

The genie folds his arms and scowls.

"You can go back to your, uh, slumber," I say. "Sorry I disturbed you."

The genie's eyebrows lower, melding together into one big eyebrow that stretches across his forehead. He doesn't look happy. "You summoned me," he says.

"Yeah," I say. "I'm sorry about that. I really didn't know you were in there." I point to the lamp. "I was just messing around."

A breeze picks up and the genie drifts a bit.

"You will make a wish," he says.

I can tell this isn't a request. I don't think anyone's ever turned this genie down before, and it's obvious he doesn't like it. He wets his lips again—his thin tongue flits out and back real quick. He hovers closer, floating almost right above me, and his eyes flash with fire.

And now I know something for sure.

This genie is no good. This genie is trouble.

There's no way I'm making a wish. A lump fills my chest, and I take a few steps back.

"Do you wish for wealth?" the genie says. He says it low and kind of threatening.

I don't say anything.

"Do you wish for fame?" he says.

He wants to destroy me. I can see that. He's been in his lamp for who knows how long, and he's dying to get back to his old business of using wishes to ruin people. That's obvious. But he can only get to me if I wish for something, so I keep my mouth shut.

"Do you wish for a special someone?" he says.

I stay quiet, but my face must give something away because the genie says, "*Ahhh!* You have but to speak her name, and she shall be yours!"

In my mind, Caroline's green eyes shine, but the truth is, I'm not even a little bit tempted. Sure, I probably ruined things with the whole *neat-o burrito* thing. But this wish, I know, would destroy me. Worse, it would destroy her, too. Because the genie's not offering love. He's offering slavery— slavery for Caroline Spencer.

I mean, suppose I do wish for her, that I blurt out the words, *I wish for Caroline Spencer!*

Then what? Just like that she's mine? I own her? She has to do whatever I say?

No. That's not what I want. That's not ... chivalrous. So I say again, "No wish for me," and I start walking.

The genie follows. His lamp stays back in the gutter.

"Wish for her," he says, floating beside me. His voice is low and dark.

"I don't want anything," I say. I turn the corner.

"Wish for her," he says again, after a few minutes. His voice is quiet but commanding.

"Leave me alone," I answer.

We pass the sandlot where the guys play baseball, Eli Turner and the others. A few call out, and I wave, knowing they can't see the genie. I trudge up my front steps and push through the door. The genie stops and seems to scowl at the doorframe, and I realize he can't come in, not unless I invite him. I realize if I step inside and close the door, I'll be free of him. He'll have to go back to his lamp, and it'll all be over.

"Wish for her," he says one last time, and his hungry eyes narrow.

"Never," I say, and it's time for him to find someone more gullible because I'm not falling for it.

I start to close the door, and the genie says, "We shall see." But then the door latches, and it's done.

I breathe. I count to ten. I check the peephole, and sure enough, he's gone. Honestly, I'm pretty proud of myself. Not everyone could have resisted a limitless wish. In the kitchen, I grab a banana and sit at the table. I think for a minute about the things I could have had—money, eternal life, my own private island to share with Caroline Spencer.

I wonder if I've done the right thing. Maybe there could have been some other way—some safe wish I could have made to end up with Caroline. Maybe I could have just wished my *neat-o burrito* away. But no. I should do things myself.

And no one—I mean, *no one*—should be wished into love. Ever.

I'm about halfway through my banana when something strange happens.

Suddenly the world kind of goes *poof*, and I'm not in my kitchen anymore. I'm back on Magnolia Avenue.

The genie is there, hovering over the fire hydrant again. I'm so freaked out I drop my banana onto the sidewalk.

"Hey," I say. "I told you I didn't want anything. I told you to leave me alone."

The genie hovers and smiles his devilish smile. His thick eyebrows come down and form the one big eyebrow, and he laughs a big, deep belly laugh.

"You, oh Matt, have been wished for," he says, grinning, and he points.

It's her. Caroline Spencer. She's holding the lamp. She's looking at me, and she's wearing this shy smile. She's finished cleaning Miss Sutherland's erasers, and on her walk home she must have seen the lamp in the gutter and picked it up.

"Hi, Matt," she says quietly, and she tucks the lamp behind her. Her green eyes flash, and suddenly I feel all numb. Something goes *click* in my head, like a light going out, and then I forget about the Red Sox and the hot dogs at Fenway Park and the catcher's mitt I got for my birthday—forever. I feel my eyes glaze over.

I forget about everything once and for all, because how could anything else possibly matter? Anything, that is, except for Caroline Spencer and her green eyes and the way she tucks her hair behind her ears when she makes comments in History class?

I mean, she's here, and I'm here. And for the rest of my life, I'll do everything she wants. I'll go everywhere she tells me. I'll get anything she asks for. Always.

Because I am hers.

I am hers.

I am hers.

CROSSING

OWEN hunched forward and tightened his backpack straps.
Today was the day.

He could feel it.

He was finally going to beat his sister, Hannah, in their weekly race. Each Monday, on their way to school, he and Hannah would toe a sidewalk crack at the bottom of Mill-hollow Hill, ready themselves, and count down...*three, two, one, go!*

And then, like fired cannonballs, they'd take off.

They'd churn their legs, pump their arms, and before they'd reach the top of the hill, some hundred yards ahead, they'd both be huffing and panting.

But always—*always!*—Hannah would win. Just barely.

It isn't fair, Owen sometimes thought. Hannah was one year and eighteen days older than him, and that made her one year and eighteen days stronger, one year and eighteen days bigger, one year and eighteen days faster.

And every Monday for years, when she crossed the finish line, marked by one of those yellow-and-black school-crossing signs, a fraction of a second before him, she chanted the exact same thing.

Girls always win! she'd say. *Girls always win!*

The crossing sign at the finish line seemed to agree with

her. There were two children on it, a girl and a boy, walking in a crosswalk, and the girl was always just slightly in front of the boy. Always a few steps faster. Always coming in first.

Just like him and Hannah.

But lately, things had been changing. He'd been gaining on Hannah, losing to her by less and less each week. He'd been getting faster and was inching his way to a win. His time was coming. He could feel it.

I can do it today, Owen thought as he and Hannah toed the line and started their countdown.

"Three!"

Owen narrowed his eyes.

"Two!"

He felt a kind of electricity in his arms and legs.

"One!"

He took in a breath and held it.

"Go!"

He burst off the sidewalk crack perfectly, getting a quicker start than Hannah. He pumped his legs, striding on his toes, trying to "run light" like Mom had taught them.

Already he was half a step ahead. Electricity seemed to crackle in the air around him. He was going to do it!

But midway up the hill, he saw Hannah out of the corner of his eye. He heard her pounding feet.

She was inching closer.

If only he could hold on...

He focused on the finish line, the boy and the girl in the

yellow diamond-shaped sign. Something about those two children pulled at Owen's eyes for just a second. The sign felt different. Wrong, even. But Owen pushed the distraction aside and told himself to go faster...*faster!*

He fought through the burning in his lungs and the aches in his legs. He focused himself. Still, Hannah crept up alongside him, and his stomach sank.

The sign was just twenty yards away. But Hannah sprang forward and edged ahead.

Come on, Owen thought, trying to catch her. *Go, go, go!*

But with only a few steps left, Hannah was definitely in front. Not by much—just a few inches. *It's her longer legs*, Owen thought, her one-year-and-eighteen-days-longer legs, taking bigger steps.

They flew past the sign. Again, something about the boy and the girl on it felt off, making Owen's skin tingle.

But the race was over.

He had lost. By inches.

He stopped, hunched forward, and rested his hands on his knees.

"Girls always win!" Hannah chanted through panting breaths. "Girls always win!"

Wait a second, Owen thought, and goose bumps rose on his arms.

He trudged back to the finish line. He stopped beside the sign's metal pole and looked up.

No way, he thought.

Because the two children in the sign, the girl and the boy, were not where they were supposed to be.

The girl was not in front.

Owen blinked and looked again, and it was true. The girl was *not* in front!

The boy was.

Owen's skin buzzed. Despite panting and sweating from the race, he felt cold all of a sudden.

"Hannah, come look at this sign," he said. "Something's strange."

"Oh, little brother," Hannah said. "There's nothing strange. I won. As usual." She blew on her fingernails and polished them on the front of her shirt.

Owen ignored her. He tried to put his most recent loss out of his head because something was definitely up. Definitely.

"I mean it." He waved Hannah back. "Come look at this."

Hannah sidled up next to him.

"Isn't that girl usually in front of that boy?" He pointed.

Hannah shrugged.

"Well, she's behind him now, see?" He waited for Hannah to say something.

She looked from him to the sign and back to him. "What's your point?" she finally said.

Owen sighed.

"My point"—he lowered his voice—"is that this sign has changed."

"Changed?" She looked at the sign again. "You get weirder every day, little brother."

But the buzzing on Owen's skin quickened. His heart thudded.

Owen tried to call up a picture of the sign from his memory. He'd passed it hundreds of times. Maybe thousands. And the girl had always been in front of the boy. Hadn't she? That was what had bothered him about the sign all these years. The girl . . . always in front. Like Hannah.

Could he have been wrong about the sign? All this time?

"So the city put up a new sign," Hannah said. "Big deal. Can we go now?"

Owen tilted his head and thought.

Hannah let out a frustrated puff of air. "If I miss another History quiz, Mom will kill me, Owen. She'll just kill me."

"But—" Owen said. And then a car stopped at the crosswalk. The driver, an older woman in a bathrobe and hair curlers, waved them across.

Hannah stepped into the street. Owen followed reluctantly, but he turned to look at the sign once more. One of its bottom corners was slightly bent, and little cracks ran all through the yellow and black paint. A small divot pockmarked the top of the sign, like it'd been hit by a rock.

Owen shook his head.

Hannah had said the sign was new. But the cracks and pockmark and bent corner told Owen the truth.

This sign was old.

—◦—

At dinner, Owen chewed his burrito slowly.

"You're quiet," his mother said.

"I'm thinking," he answered. He considered telling her about the sign, asking her which kid was supposed to be in front on a school-crossing sign, the boy or the girl, but he didn't want to bring it up again in front of Hannah. She'd tell him he was acting crazy, and she might even tell their parents that she'd beaten him—yet again—that morning. So he decided to stay silent.

Maybe Hannah was right after all, and the sign had been replaced—not with a new sign, but with an old sign, a recycled one. But would the city have done that?

Or maybe something was happening. Something strange. Maybe that boy, now in front, was a kind of...prediction... or a premonition. Yes, that was the word. A premonition of things to come.

Of him, finally winning.

He shook his head and gulped down his milk.

No, he told himself. *That's crazy*. More likely, he'd just been wrong about the sign for years. Probably the boy had always been walking in front, and he'd been seeing it wrong all this time. That was all.

Owen closed his eyes. He tried picturing the sign, going back to his memories to get a clear view of it. But everything felt fuzzy. Confused.

Which kid was supposed to be in front in a school crossing sign? The boy? The girl?

Thinking about it, Owen could see it both ways.

⁓

The next morning, Owen hooked his thumbs in his backpack straps and walked quickly up Millhollow Hill.

"Hey, wait up," Hannah said as Owen pulled away. "It's not a race day, you know."

At the top of the hill, Owen stopped. In the sign, the girl was in front of the boy.

The girl was back in front of the boy!

They had switched! Again! It couldn't be!

"Hannah," Owen said. "Think hard. Is this what we saw on this sign yesterday?"

"You've got to be kidding me," Hannah said.

Owen spoke low and tried to make his voice sound serious.

"I think this sign keeps changing," Owen said.

Hannah rolled her eyes.

"Doesn't that bother you?"

Hannah shrugged. She didn't even look at the sign. "Your mind's playing tricks on you, Owen. That's all. It's just a street sign. So no, it doesn't bother me. What does bother me is missing History quizzes."

Hannah stepped off the curb and crossed the street. But Owen was sure of it now. He wasn't seeing things wrong. Or remembering them wrong.

Those two children in the faded, flaking sign—that boy and that girl—they could move.

———

For the rest of the week, each time Owen passed the sign, his skin tingled. He didn't know if the sign was trying to give him a prediction or a premonition or something else altogether, but the sign did seem to be giving off some kind of radiation, like a beacon, signaling him.

Each time he passed it, he took a mental picture of what he saw.

On Wednesday, the girl was in front, but the book she usually carried was on the ground next to her. Her head was bent, and she seemed to be reaching for it.

On Thursday, the book was back in her hands, but now she was behind the boy.

And on Friday, the boy was holding her book.

Each day, the sign made some small change, and each day, Hannah refused to talk about it.

"It's a stupid sign, Owen!" she'd said, throwing her hands up the last time he'd mentioned it.

No matter how much he begged, Owen couldn't even get her to look at the sign. He'd begun to wonder if *anyone* looked at it besides him.

The next Monday, he toed the sidewalk crack next to Hannah, and he tried to put the sign out of his head. But he couldn't help peering at it, a hundred yards ahead. He couldn't make out the boy and girl from so far away, so he couldn't see just how they'd changed this time.

While he was still squinting ahead, Hannah started the countdown.

"Three, two, one, go!"

She burst ahead right from the start.

No, he thought. *Not again.*

He hadn't been ready. He'd been so distracted by the sign that he'd forgotten to tighten his backpack straps, so he ran, and his backpack flumped on his shoulders. He churned his legs. He pumped his arms. But it was no use.

He never even got close to Hannah.

She beat him by at least five steps.

Instead of running hard through the finish, Owen slowed and stopped beneath the sign. He slid his backpack off his shoulders and dropped it to the sidewalk. The boy and the girl were back to normal. The girl in front. The boy a few steps behind. The sign was ordinary. Regular.

"This again?" Hannah said. "Owen, you're imagining things."

"I'm not." Owen shook his head. "But you can go on ahead. Go take your History quiz."

Owen touched the sign's cool metal pole.

"Whatever," Hannah said. "Oh, and by the way, girls

always win." She stepped off the curb and crossed the street. When she was far enough away, Owen spoke.

"I see you," he said to the boy and the girl. "I know you're in there."

He waited. The sign did nothing.

"Move," he said, but the sign was just a sign. "Come on, move."

Nothing happened.

"What are you?" The late bell rang.

Owen sighed and picked up his backpack. He took two steps, turned, and peered at the sign one last time.

He choked on his breath.

They'd moved—the boy and the girl. Right as he'd been standing there.

The girl was hunched in a low corner now, squatting. The boy stood behind her, and their arms seemed to be reaching out . . . to him.

"You want something," Owen said, moving back to the sign. "Is that it? You're trapped in there, and there's something you need?"

Owen raised up on his toes. He stretched one arm. The sign was just within his reach . . . but before he touched one of the girl's outstretched arms, he thought that maybe he shouldn't.

For a week, the sign had been beckoning him. It had started when it had shown him a boy in front. Even now he felt the sign coaxing him nearer and nearer. Why?

But he couldn't stop himself. He had to touch the sign. It was all so strange. So impossible. He just had to. So pushing past his fear, he reached up and pressed a finger to the girl's tiny, reaching hand.

At once, the world spun and twisted. His ears filled with a windy, whooshing sound. Colors blurred. And for a moment, Owen struggled to breathe. Everything tottered from side to side.

Then his world turned to yellow and black.

—◦—

After school, Hannah passed the sign on her way home. She'd waited for Owen by the flagpole like always, but he hadn't shown up. Maybe he'd ditched her, still upset about losing that morning.

She didn't even glance at the sign as she strolled by it, even though Owen had been completely obsessed with it lately. Why should she? It was just a dumb sign.

But if she had looked, here is what she would have seen:

Three children pacing through a crosswalk.

A girl...and two boys.

One of the boys was shinier than the other two children, newer, as if he had been painted on just that morning.

And it was this boy, glossy and new, who was out in front of the other two children.

Finally coming in first.

THE VOICE

SOMETHING *would have to be done about Mrs. Huber,* Cindy thought. *Something drastic.* The school year was four months old now, and while Mrs. Huber didn't assign too much homework or force students to do group projects, Cindy found her methods to be...problematic.

It was Mrs. Huber's voice—the way she yelled so much— that bothered Cindy.

What to do, what to do? she thought.

She ran a finger along the shelf of old books that her grandmother had left her. She had a few ideas, but nothing definite. Nothing that had really taken shape.

One thing was certain though.

It was time for someone to stop Mrs. Huber. Someone with power.

⌐ ━

"Silence!" Mrs. Huber screamed.

Her voice came out high-pitched and shrill, a bit like a cackling witch—exactly the way she'd intended.

Her twenty-seven students fell instantly quiet. They even stopped moving, widening their eyes and freezing at their desks with their pencils poised above their worksheets. Only the clock on the wall made a sound, and Mrs. Huber paused while it went *tick, tick, tick.*

"There will be no more talking today!" she continued, and the students stayed statue-still.

A warmth swelled inside Mrs. Huber, and she let it build and fill her up.

Perfect, she thought. *This is perfect.*

It hadn't been easy, developing the perfect teacher voice. It had taken years—more than her gray head cared to remember—to get it just right. But now, after teaching sixth grade for what seemed like forever, she'd mastered it.

The Voice.

It was the only thing that made it possible for her to endure middle-schoolers at all.

The Voice could make students do anything.

It could bring a running hallway delinquent to a sneaker-skidding halt. It could send goo-goo-eyed hand holders on the softball field scampering in different directions. It could even silence an entire auditorium of gossiping students. And now, in her own class, when she'd wanted silence, it had brought all twenty-seven of her students to a graveyard-quiet stop.

Perfect.

"You will spend the last seven minutes of class reading in absolute silence!" Mrs. Huber said, softening *The Voice* just a little, but not too much. "You will not daydream! You will not whisper to your neighbor! And you will not doodle in your margins! Is that clear?"

Twenty-seven sixth graders nodded in unison.

"Good," she said, bringing *The Voice* down to a low, raspy hiss. "Because if you do, I'll burn your ears with my words." She spoke this threat often, and when she did, she let her words hang in the air like a thick fog.

Her students opened their books gently, the way people opened magazines in quiet waiting rooms. Mrs. Huber smiled. Then she sat at her own desk and opened her book—*The Fall of the Roman Empire.* She pretended to read, but really she focused on the satisfied warmth swelling inside her. It felt so good to have control! She remembered her first few teaching years, before she'd mastered *The Voice.* They'd been so chaotic, so disordered. Students had shouted. They'd passed notes. They'd doodled.

But there's none of that now, she thought as she crossed her legs, leaned back in her chair, and sighed.

Just then, out of the corner of her eye, she sensed something that wasn't... right.

Someone in her class was acting differently. At the edge of her sight, someone's head was straight up and stiff-necked, not hunched over a book at all. Mrs. Huber turned.

It was Cindy Watson, a small girl with mousy brown hair.

Mrs. Huber opened her mouth, but no words came out. She didn't understand. Cindy Watson had never caused any trouble before. She turned her homework in on time. She sat with good posture at her desk. She did her worksheets in perfect silence. But as Mrs. Huber narrowed her eyes, there was no doubt about it.

Cindy Watson was not reading.

Somehow she was defying *The Voice*.

There was a book on her desk. It had a dark blue cover and a title Mrs. Huber couldn't make out, but it wasn't even open. Cindy was looking straight ahead with a blank expression, as if she were daydreaming out a window—only there were no windows in Mrs. Huber's classroom, just solid, blank walls.

Mrs. Huber closed her own book and flung it onto her desk. *How*, Mrs. Huber thought, *could this be happening?* She stood up and glared at Cindy. The girl seemed not to notice.

I can fix this, thought Mrs. Huber. *I can fix this now.* She cleared her throat. She opened her mouth, filling her lungs with air, and prepared to use *The Voice* at one hundred percent strength.

Just then, the bell rang, and before Mrs. Huber could speak, Cindy shuffled out of the room to lunch along with the other students.

Mrs. Huber exhaled, and air wheezed out of her as if she were a deflating balloon.

She walked to Cindy's desk. Her book was still on it, unopened and placed carefully at the desk's center. It was a classic. *The Witch of Blackbird Pond.*

Witch. It was a word Mrs. Huber knew all too well. It was the same word her students whispered when her back was turned. Usually, she didn't mind this a bit. In fact, she kind of liked being called a witch. The more witchy her students thought she was, the more afraid of her they would be.

But this book—*The Witch of Blackbird Pond*—centered on Cindy's desk right after she'd resisted *The Voice*, was too much. It was too bold—as if Cindy was calling Mrs. Huber a witch, not in a whispered voice behind her back, but right to her face.

How rude! How disrespectful!

Mrs. Huber swiped at Cindy's book and sent it to the floor with a *smack.*

How could Cindy, mousy little Cindy, have done this?

Minutes later, Mrs. Huber pushed her way to the cafeteria.

"Move," she yelled, using *The Voice* at full strength. A crowd of children pressed themselves against the hallway walls to let her pass.

Mrs. Huber hadn't set foot in the cafeteria for longer than she could remember. Why, after all, would she want to watch her students eat? They had the manners of cave dwellers. Besides, the lunch hour was *her* time—her time to sit and think and be away from them and their loud voices and loud hairstyles and loud clothes.

But today Mrs. Huber stomped into a corner of the cafeteria, stood straight-backed by the wall, and scanned the tables. She needed to find Cindy Watson. Not to talk to her. To study her.

Know your enemy, she reminded herself. This was a bit of wisdom she'd picked up early in her teaching career. Now seemed the right time to remember it.

Since Mrs. Huber had perfected *The Voice*, not one student—not *one*—had disobeyed her.

Until Cindy.

How?

There had to be an explanation.

"Your ears will burn for this, Cindy Watson," she muttered to herself. "They will sizzle, and they will burn."

She scanned the cafeteria. She ignored the lunchroom smells—overprocessed meats mixed with too many growing bodies. She lowered her glasses and peered over them.

Suddenly a voice interrupted her.

"I'm glad to see you here, Barbara." It was Principal Garcia. Mrs. Huber let out a little puff of air. She hated being called *Barbara*, especially around students. She was *Mrs. Huber*. "It's good for the students to see us outside of class," the principal went on. "It lets them know we're human."

He smiled.

Mrs. Huber didn't.

The week before, Principal Garcia had called her into his office to talk about her *tendency to speak a bit forcefully*.

Mrs. Huber let out another little puff. This was Principal Garcia's first year as a middle-school principal, and he had all kinds of "fresh" ideas about teaching. Eventually, she figured, he'd learn what really worked on children. But for now he was hopelessly bright-eyed and bushy-tailed.

"I'm not changing my methods," she'd told him that day. "I'm controlling my class—perfectly, in fact—and instead of calling me in here to ask me to *change*, you should be *thanking* me, young man." She'd stood up when she'd told him this. "When you're ready to show me *appreciation* for that, I'll be in my classroom."

She'd stormed out of his office, and she hadn't spoken to him since. Now, in the cafeteria, Principal Garcia smiled at her like everything was fine. He put one hand in his pocket as if he were searching for something there, but just then, some student across the cafeteria called out, "Yo, Garcia-man!" and Principal Garcia smiled brightly, waved at the student, and walked toward him to give him a high five.

Mrs. Huber shook her head. She'd never thought she would see a principal high-fiving students or letting them speak so savagely. *Yo, Garcia-man?* It was repulsive.

Mrs. Huber sighed and went back to her search for Cindy.

Where are you? she thought. She scanned the near side of the cafeteria.

Just then, someone by the soda machines dropped a lunch tray. It clattered to the tile floor. Mrs. Huber turned, along with everyone else, to see who'd done it.

It wasn't Cindy Watson, sadly.

It would have served her right, Mrs. Huber thought.

But it was André Parker, the shortest boy in her class. He was standing over his lunch, a mess of french fries and a facedown slice of pizza, his cheeks the color of raspberries.

One boy called out, "Smooth move, André!" and a few other kids clapped.

Mrs. Huber shook her head.

They were such a mess, these kids. No manners at all. No dignity.

Then Mrs. Huber found Cindy Watson. She was walking across the cafeteria, holding her lunch tray. Mrs. Huber pushed her glasses up. It was time to concentrate. How had Cindy resisted *The Voice*? What was so special about her?

Cindy walked toward André, who was on his knees gathering his mess. When Cindy reached him, she touched his shoulder. Then she crouched down and helped him clean up the last of his scattered french fries.

Mrs. Huber's legs went slightly weak.

She didn't understand it. This girl was the one who could defy *The Voice*?

André and Cindy stood. Cindy lifted her plate of french fries and pizza off her tray and held it out to André.

André shook his head shyly, but Cindy smiled, said something, and put the plate on André's tray. Then she turned and walked away.

Mrs. Huber couldn't understand it.

How? she thought.

Cindy Watson was the first disobedient student she had taught in years—*in years*! Of all the students who wanted to defy her, how could it be gentle Cindy Watson who had succeeded?

Mrs. Huber's hands started shaking.

This wasn't a rebellious girl. She didn't wear black clothes or have strange piercings. She didn't dye her hair blue or break the school dress code. She was the only student who had helped André Parker. The only one.

And yet somehow she had resisted *The Voice*. And if mousy little Cindy could resist...

Mrs. Huber didn't finish her thought.

She stormed toward the cafeteria doors. Principal Garcia was standing nearby, laughing with a group of students.

"Come again, Barbara," he said as she passed, and he slipped a hand into his pocket and seemed to want to say more.

She ignored him and burst into the faculty lounge, where she tore her lunch from the fridge.

Cindy Watson must be punished! she thought.

Cindy had been disobedient. It didn't matter whether or not she looked like a rebel. She had been told to read quietly— in the clearest of terms—and she hadn't. It was that simple. What she had just done for André Parker didn't excuse that.

Mrs. Huber pulled a stalk of celery from her lunch bag.

If she let this girl defy her, there would be others. There would be chaos: passed notes and blurted comments and chronic lateness.

Yes, Mrs. Huber thought. *Cindy Watson must be stopped.*

She snapped the stick of celery in half.

After lunch, she'd have to confront Cindy. In front of everyone. She would have to use *The Voice* at its fullest strength. Mrs. Huber crunched her celery.

Even if Cindy resisted at first, like she had before, she'd give in to *The Voice* eventually. Everyone did. It was like magic.

Besides, reducing Cindy to rubble—making her weaken and wobble in front of all the others—would be a good reminder to everyone that no one was safe in her class. No one. Not even the "nice" kids.

She finished her lunch and clopped down the hallway. She almost smiled, thinking of the lesson that was soon to come for Cindy and for everyone else.

Do not challenge Mrs. Huber.

When her students trickled into her classroom, she'd burn that lesson into their ears. Forever.

———

She pushed through her classroom door and checked the clock. There were three minutes before the bell would ring and the students would start filtering in. *The Witch of Black-bird Pond* lay on the floor by Cindy's desk. Mrs. Huber bent to pick it up, but stopped short—

Cindy could pick up her book herself.

Mrs. Huber sat at her desk and waited. She breathed slowly in and out. She cleared her throat.

And that was when she saw the note. It was on a small white card and had been placed on her desk just next to her stapler. The note said:

Mrs. Huber,
For all you've done, you deserve this.

There was no signature, but next to the note there was a small black box. It was the kind that usually held jewelry.

Mrs. Huber picked it up.

Finally, she thought. *Someone appreciates me.*

She remembered Principal Garcia in the cafeteria—his friendly words and the way he'd seemed to want to say more. He'd even reached into his pants pocket, like he'd been about to pull something out, hadn't he? Something maybe the size of a jewelry box?

The man has finally come to his senses, she thought. *He's apologizing.* He must have brought his apology gift here while she'd been in the faculty lounge eating. Too bad he didn't have the guts to apologize in person, the weasel.

She fingered the note. She opened the box.

Earrings glittered beneath the classroom lights, gold ones with tiny hoops. Her mouth opened slightly. They were fancier than the simple jewelry Mrs. Huber usually wore, and she plucked them out of the box.

Why shouldn't she enjoy a reward for all her hard work over the years? She removed the silver studs in her ears and put the new earrings on. They swung slightly from her earlobes.

Principal Garcia is still doing everything wrong, she thought. *But maybe there is hope for him.* When she saw him next, she'd nod and point to the earrings, and then she'd go on using *The Voice* as she always had.

The bell rang, and the students began to trickle in. After a minute, Cindy walked in and sat straight-postured at her desk.

Mrs. Huber didn't say anything. Not yet. She wanted everyone to be present when she began. She wanted all her students to see.

The late bell rang, and a straggler, Jayden Moore, speed-walked from the classroom door to his seat. Mrs. Huber stood. The class became silent. Her new earrings sent light dancing across the walls. She paced the front of the classroom. Twenty-seven sets of eyes followed her.

Cindy Watson, Mrs. Huber thought. *A storm is coming for you, little mouse.* She almost felt bad for Cindy. Almost. The girl was still just sitting straight-backed at her desk with her hands in her lap, half smiling. She had no idea what was coming. No idea at all.

Mrs. Huber stopped in front of Cindy's desk. She paused. She pointed to *The Witch of Blackbird Pond*, which was still on the floor. She took in a breath of air and tightened the muscles in her neck, readying *The Voice*.

Cindy Watson! Stand! Now! she yelled.

Or that's what she'd planned to do.

What really happened was this:

"Cin—" she yelled, and then she stopped and bent over and covered her ears. When the first syllable shot out of her mouth, her ears had grown suddenly hot.

They burned white and strong, and the unexpected pain silenced her instantly. After a second, the burning stopped.

She touched her ears and felt the new earrings dangling there.

She tried again.

"Cin—" she yelled, and this time the pain was blinding. Heat flashed like an explosion in her ears. It was as if her earlobes were being dipped in boiling water, and she winced and lurched forward. Again, as soon as she stopped speaking, the pain faded.

Her students looked at her, waiting.

Mrs. Huber couldn't understand it. What was happening?

She tried again, lowering *The Voice* slightly. But once more, as the first syllable left her mouth, her ears burned and she had to stop speaking.

She tried whispering. Even that seared her earlobes, and she thought she heard tiny hisses.

The earrings, she realized. Principal Garcia had done something.

She reached up to her left ear and tried to remove the earring. She grabbed the back clasp and pulled, but the earring wouldn't unlatch. She tried her right earring, but the same thing happened. It was as if the earrings had fused permanently to her ears.

She ran to her desk and fumbled for the earring box. She read the card again:

For all you've done, you deserve this.

The Voice, she thought. She looked at her students with sinking eyes.

"Mrs. Huber, is something wrong?" said Johnny Pak without raising his hand. But that couldn't be. Her students always raised their hands.

"Yeah, you don't look so good," said Amira Cox. She stood up by her desk.

"Should I get the nurse?" blurted Sharon Cross.

There was a pause. Mrs. Huber's earlobes pulsed. She didn't dare speak. She shook her head slightly, and then Bobbie Duncan called out in a loud voice:

"Hey, there's something wrong with Mrs. Huber!"

Then, all at once, the children were talking. Loudly. They fluttered. They buzzed. The noises they made swelled and rose, and the kids in the back of the room even stood on their chairs to see what was happening. Connor Davis, in the very back row, jumped up and stood on his desk.

"Get back in—" she started to say, but as she spoke, the heat in her ears flared, and the shock of it silenced her once more.

She pulled at the earrings. She tugged at her earlobes. Nothing worked. The noise in the room became deafening.

Around her, twenty-seven students bounced and buzzed and yelled.

But no, she realized. It wasn't twenty-seven.

It was twenty-six.

One student—Cindy Watson—sat in her chair, statue-still. In all the chaos, she'd picked her book up, and she was reading it, silently, with a crooked smile.

Witch *is such a misunderstood word*, thought Cindy. Her classmates—the same ones yelling and jostling just then for a better look at their flailing teacher—had used that word dozens of times to describe Mrs. Huber.

What a ridiculous idea, Cindy thought. *Mrs. Huber a witch!*

Cindy sighed and turned a page in her book.

It just proved what Cindy's grandmother always told her.

Most people knew nothing about witches. Nothing.

Goodbye, Ridgecrest Middle School

IT was during the five-minute break between Mr. Johansen's Science class and Mr. Johnson's English class. Wally was in the bathroom washing his hands and practicing his teachers' names.

Johnson. Johansen.

He lathered soap between his fingers.

It was one of those cruel tricks of the universe, he thought, one of those little ways it was out to get him. Why else would he have two teachers with virtually identical names?

Just a few minutes earlier, he'd had a conversation that went like this:

"Hey, Mr. Johnson?"

"It's Jo-*HAN*-sen, Wally. For the last time, Jo-*HAN*-sen. Get it right."

"Oh, yeah. Sorry."

It was an understandable mistake, Wally had thought, but Mr. Johansen had turned away, clacked his chalk hard onto the metal chalk holder, and Wally never got the chance to ask his question.

Wally turned off the bathroom tap and muttered "Mr. Johnson. Mr. Johansen" over and over in a low voice, but he knew repeating the names wouldn't help. Those two names had become like tangled ropes in his head, and he wasn't entirely sure he had them right even now.

He shook his dripping hands and waved them in front of the paper towel dispenser's red blinking eye.

Nothing happened. The paper that normally came spooling out, didn't.

"Great," said Wally, thinking again of the out-to-get-him universe. "Piece of junk's broken."

He tried again, waving at the blinking red eye more slowly. His wet hands glistened, and a single drop of water fell from his left pinkie onto his shoe with a *plop*. Finally the machine whirred. A scratchy-looking sheet of paper scrolled out.

Wally stopped.

Before him, on the dangling page, was something Wally couldn't explain.

Words.

They were written in a dark, thick scrawl and said:

YOU HAVE TWO DAYS LEFT

Weird, thought Wally. The words looked angry. The letters were jagged and seemed to have been pressed hard into the paper.

"Two days left?" Wally mumbled. He tore the paper away, wadded it into a ball, and dropped it into the trash. Then he waved his hand in front of the dispenser again. The machine whirred. A piece of paper scrolled out, and the words appeared again:

YOU HAVE TWO DAYS LEFT

Wally peered through the dispenser's gray semi-transparent cover. Inside, he could make out a big spool of paper and a few gears. Nothing else. The paper on the spool seemed blank.

Wally tore the second sheet of paper from the dispenser. He held it up and examined it under the light.

Just then, Brandon Reynolds pushed through the bathroom door. Wally crumpled the paper as Brandon stepped up to a urinal.

Wally tossed the paper into the garbage can. He wanted to see what would happen when Brandon waved his hands in front of the blinking eye—if the words would show up on his paper, too—so he waited and leaned in close to the mirror and pretended to look at something on his face. He ran his fingers through his hair. He hunched and untied and retied his shoelaces.

Finally Brandon flushed, washed, and waved the backs of his dripping hands in front of the red eye. A section of paper scrolled out.

There was nothing. No words. Just an empty sheet. Brandon ripped it off, dried his hands, and left.

Wally walked to the dispenser. Slowly, he waved his hand

in front of the red eye. The machine whirred, and the words appeared again:

YOU HAVE TWO DAYS LEFT

Wally swallowed hard. Whatever this dispenser was saying, it seemed to be saying it only to him. Whatever fate loomed on the horizon, it was his.

Two days left? Two days left for *what*?

Suddenly the whole Johnson-Johansen thing didn't seem so important.

The universe, it seemed, really was out to get him.

———

Two days left could mean anything, Wally thought as he lay in his bed that night.

Maybe he had just two days left to finish his science project. Or maybe he had just two days left of lunch money on his school account. Maybe this was some kind of elaborate reminder a teacher had set up to keep kids on track for an assignment. After all, it did sort of feel like something Mr. Johnson would do.

Or was it something Mr. Johansen would do?

Wally shook his head. It didn't matter because those words—*You have two days left*—didn't mean anything. They were part of a prank or a joke or a trick. That was all.

Still, Wally squirmed under his covers, and in his head, the words kept scrolling before his eyes.

Two days left.
Two days left.
Two days left.

— —

By the next morning, Wally had convinced himself it was probably nothing.

Yes, it's definitely nothing, he told himself as he shoveled a spoonful of Twisty-Ohs into his mouth.

Paper towel dispensers couldn't know things, things like how many days you had left to... well... whatever. And even if they could, they couldn't tell you about it.

In the night, he'd come up with a new theory to explain what was happening.

It had to be the school janitor, Jerry Robinson. He was an old man with gray skin that stretched tight across his arms and face. He was always smiling and playing pranks—like dropping fake vomit in the busiest hallways and laughing as kids scrambled past. He was probably the person who loaded new paper into the bathroom dispensers when they ran out. Wally spooned more cereal into his mouth.

Yes, it must have been Jerry, he told himself. Wally could just see the old janitor in his coveralls, hunched over a heavy roll of paper, smirking and scribbling those messages with a black marker.

Very funny, Jerry, Wally thought. *Ha-ha.*

To prove his point, when he got to school, Wally ignored

the morning bell and walked to the bathroom. His feet made soft tapping sounds on the tile floor. He went straight to the paper towel dispenser. He stood before it for a few seconds and then checked under the stalls to make sure no one else was in the bathroom.

The dispenser's red eye blinked, and Wally raised a shaking hand and waved. The machine whirred. Paper scrolled out:

YOU HAVE ONE DAY LEFT

Wally stared.

How is this happening? he thought.

He waved again, and more paper spooled:

YOU HAVE ONE DAY LEFT

He peered into the dispenser. The roll of paper inside was blank. He waved again . . . and again. Each time he did, paper scrolled and the same five words appeared.

Wally paced in front of the sinks.

He should ignore this. He knew that. He should ignore this and get to class. But Wally couldn't. He returned to the dispenser and waved his hand. He couldn't stop.

The paper kept coming—always with the same words. Between waves, Wally stopped ripping the sheets off individually. He let one long sheet pile up on the floor at his feet.

This can't be happening, Wally thought. *There's no way this can be happening.*

Wally's chest began to pound. His cheeks grew hot.

Just one day left, he thought. *How could that be?* He was only a kid.

One day left.

One day left.

He wanted so much more than one day.

He scooped up the long stretch of paper from the floor and tore it. The ripping sound it made was the only thing that seemed to make any sense, the only thing that felt right.

So he ripped at the paper again. He crumpled sheets and flung shreds. He threw them to the floor and kicked at them. He grabbed for the largest pieces and tore them smaller, and soon the floor was covered in wrinkled paper.

The late bell rang.

Wally stopped.

He stood in the center of the bathroom, surrounded by a ring of debris.

"One day left," he muttered, and he left the bathroom, not bothering to clean up any of his mess.

He didn't listen to his teachers that day—not Mr. Johnson or Mr. Johansen or any of the others. Why should he?

Instead, he sat at his desk, not talking to anyone. There was so much he wanted to do, but knowing he had just one day left, he couldn't find the will to do anything. It was like that dispenser in the bathroom had sucked the life out of him.

That night, he skipped his homework and his chores and dug his stash of Halloween candy out from under his bed. He'd planned to save it, to eat it little by little, slowly enough to make it last the entire year, but what was the point now? He ate as much candy as his stomach would hold—suckers, chocolate bars, taffy. His belly bulged, and he developed a headache from all the sugar, but he unwrapped another chocolate-covered toffee and shoved it in anyway.

One day left, he thought.

He hadn't told anybody what was going to happen. Not even his parents. He couldn't see the point. Most likely they'd think he was crazy. And if they didn't, they wouldn't be able to stop what was coming anyway.

Because when the universe was out to get you...it got you. Period. There was no stopping it.

Besides, his friends and his parents would find out soon enough. Why should he make them worry?

He closed his eyes—finally too tired to stay awake munching candy—and he saw, as if tattooed on his eyelids, the bathroom dispenser's red eye, blinking and blinking and blinking.

He woke. To his surprise, he got dressed and went to school. He didn't quite understand why, but he actually wanted to see Ridgecrest Middle School one last time. To say goodbye, he guessed.

"Are you okay, Wally?" people kept asking. "You look a little strange."

"I'm fine, Mr. Johnson," he answered during third period.

"I'm Mr. Jo-HAN-sen, Wally." The teacher closed his eyes and sighed. "Mr. *Jo-HAN-sen*."

Wally shrugged.

After class, he walked slowly to the bathroom. He didn't particularly want to see the dispenser, but if today really was his last day, he felt he needed to face it.

When he walked in, a piece of paper was already dangling from the dispenser. It said:

IT HAppENS TODAY

Wally read the words over and over, and something inside him snapped.

It's not fair, he thought.

There were so many things he still wanted to do. He wanted to drive a car. He wanted to eat lots of cake. He wanted to stay up all night watching movies—at least fifty more times. And he wanted to ride a motorcycle. He'd never even touched a motorcycle, he realized.

He thought of how it might happen. He'd avoided thinking about that all this time, but he couldn't avoid it anymore.

He didn't have a cough or the stomach flu or even any aches, so he figured he wasn't going to get sick. Probably, he would end up in some kind of accident. Would he get hit by a car on his way home? Would that be it? Or would he choke on a piece of lousy school pizza? Would it be his very last meal?

He was starting to shake thinking about it.

I hope it happens quickly, he thought.

And then he added, *I hope it doesn't hurt.*

He walked to the paper towel dispenser, tore the paper off, and slapped one hand hard against the dispenser.

"I didn't want to know this," Wally said, crumpling the paper. "Why would anyone want to know this?"

As if in answer, the red eye blinked. Without his waving for it, a sheet of paper scrolled out:

IT HAPPENS TODAY

Wally leaned toward the dispenser.

"I know," he said in an angry whisper.

It wasn't fair. The blinking red eye had chosen him. Why? Why him? The red eye floated there blinking, blinking, blinking.

Wally balled a fist and punched the dispenser. Hard. The

punch cracked the plastic cover, and sent a few plastic shards to the floor.

The impact hurt Wally's knuckles. But what did it matter? It felt good to hit this thing that had been coming for him, so he punched again, and more cracks spider-webbed across the dispenser's plastic cover.

He leaned in, punching harder this time, and he broke through the plastic cover, putting a fist-sized hole in the dispenser. The shattered plastic cut him, and his knuckles started bleeding.

Big deal, he thought. *So what?*

Then the dispenser whirred and a fresh piece of paper scrolled out. Wally waited for the message—*It happens today*—to appear.

It didn't.

The message came...

But one word had changed:

IT HAPPENS NOW

Wally started shaking.

"Now?" he said, and something inside him burst.

He went wild, striking and flailing and ripping at the paper. He swung a leg up and kicked the dispenser, and a loud *crash* echoed in the tiled bathroom.

He screamed and sent a few more kicks at the dispenser.

Then he grabbed the whole thing and pulled until he tore it off the wall with a loud *crack*. *It happens now*, the dispenser had said. How much time did he have? Ten seconds? Less? He threw the dispenser to the floor and stomped. Plastic shards flew. The paper roll spooled out, and Wally stomped it again and again, crushing it.

It felt good to use his final moments to get back at this thing, this thing that had set out to get him.

He shattered what he could. He dented anything that wouldn't break. He smashed and smashed, until the sound of his rampage was like an echoing jackhammer.

Soon the dispenser was nothing but fragments. In the mess, he sought out what was left of the eye. Somehow it was still flickering and fizzling with its last hints of life.

"STOP!"

Wally turned toward the booming voice.

It was his Science teacher, Mr. Whatever-His-Name-Was, his hands balled into fists at his sides, his face glowing an angry purple.

"What are you doing?" he shouted.

"I'm doing *this*!" Wally said, kicking at a plastic shard. The teacher's eyes narrowed to small slits.

The crushed roll of paper wobbled near Wally's feet, so he bent and picked it up. "And I'm doing *this*!" He raised the paper roll over his head and brought it down as fast and hard as he could onto the floor.

"Enough!" the teacher bellowed, and Wally kicked two

more times at the floor before he stopped. He was panting a little now that it was over—now that everything was almost over. The dispenser was a shattered mess, and even if it was his last second on earth, Wally felt better. At least he'd gotten rid of the thing. At least he was taking it with him.

The teacher walked farther into the bathroom and surveyed the disaster. His purple face pulsed.

"I can't believe you did this," he said, shaking his head. "Wally, I cannot believe you did this."

Wally pointed down. "Mr. Johnson," he said, "that thing—"

"My name," the teacher interrupted in a low voice as he moved closer to Wally, "is Mr. Jo-HAN-sen. And you're going to remember it this time, Wally, because after all this"—he waved an arm around the room—"I'm the teacher who'll make sure you never set foot in Ridgecrest Middle School ever again."

Wally's eyes widened.

"This will be your last day here," Mr. Johansen hissed. "Your very last day."

Oh, thought Wally, feeling a strange mix of relief and dread. On the floor, near his foot, a red light flickered and went out forever.

MIGHTY COMFY

WE were on our way home from my volleyball practice, driving down Harris Street in Dad's truck, when Dad hit the brakes hard enough that my seat belt locked up.

"Heidi!" he said. "Check out that couch! It's practically brand-new!" Dad pointed to a brown couch that sat along the curb between two elm trees. It was big and squashy and had short dark legs. A cardboard sign on it read: FREE TO A GOOD HOME.

This happened all the time in our neighborhood. People just left stuff on their curbs for others to take. We'd gotten a bunch of furniture this way—a coffee table and a dresser and two barstools. It was one of the reasons Dad drove a truck. We could always load stuff up.

"I can't believe the things people get rid of," Dad said with a smile. He opened his door and hopped out.

I rolled down my window.

"This will look great in the TV room." Dad circled the couch a few times. Dad loved his TV room. He spent practically every minute in there watching old westerns. John Wayne was his favorite.

"Aw, Dad," I said, "are you sure we want that old thing?"

It wasn't like we needed all this free furniture. We weren't poor or anything. The problem was Dad could never resist.

He even brought home two church pews once—*church pews!* He lined them up along the sides of his TV room even though we already had enough seating for the three people in our house—me, Dad, and Mom. We tripped over the pews for days before Mom finally convinced the Wallaces up the street to take them.

I leaned out the truck window and wondered what sorts of things had been on that couch. Crusty food? Flea-ridden animals? Something worse?

"Uh, Dad." I spoke quietly. "Whoever put that couch here probably had a good reason for getting rid of it," I said, trying to change his mind.

"What do you mean, little pardner?" Dad looked up from the couch.

Little pardner. It was one of my nicknames. I had a lot of them, all from Dad's westerns. There was also Dead-Eye, Slim, and Wrangler.

Dad eyed the couch again and his smile lit up like a billboard. A find like this made him really happy.

"I don't know," I said. "Maybe the couch has bugs...or lice...or germs."

Dad leaned in and smelled the couch. He slapped the cushions a few times and studied the dust that swirled up.

"I don't think so," he said. "This couch is great. It's perfect."

He plopped down onto it, and I shivered a little. I opened the truck door and jumped out.

"People these days throw stuff out way too soon, Heidi-o."

He took a deep breath. "Back in the day, people hung on to things. They had to back then."

Dad talked a lot about the "good old days," but he didn't mean when he was a kid. He meant the Wild West days—the days from his movies.

"Well, Slick," Dad said, "help me load it up."

Dad lifted one end of the couch, and I tried to lift the other. It was heavier than we expected, so I kind of had to nudge and slide my end, but after a few minutes, we muscled the couch into the back of the truck, and Dad slammed the tailgate. I wiped my hands on my shorts.

"Your mom will be thrilled," he said. I wasn't so sure about that, but Dad just beamed.

When we got home, we had to rearrange a lot of furniture to make space for the couch. We had to push the recliners against the far wall and shift the coffee table over by the fireplace. When there was an open spot, we put the couch right in the middle of the TV room, just like Dad wanted.

Mom raised her eyebrows. "I don't know," she said, shaking her head. "Do we really need it?"

"It's perfect," Dad said. He clapped his hands twice and looked at me. "Didn't I tell you it'd be perfect?"

Mom pulled the vacuum out and started swiping away at the couch with the hand attachment. "You never know where these things have been," she said.

When she switched the vacuum off, Dad plopped down on the couch and turned on the TV. The cushions were big and fluffy, and Dad sank down into them. He reached for his cowboy hat, a big, brown Stetson he kept on the coffee table and only wore while he watched his westerns.

"Perfect," he said. "I'll spend hours on this baby." He patted the couch like it was a new pet. He clicked the remote and flipped through the channels. "Mighty comfy," he said.

A few seconds later, he pointed to the TV.

"What luck! This is *Rio Bravo*," he said. On the screen, a smiling John Wayne polished a star-shaped badge on his vest. "It's a classic! John Wayne plays a sheriff. It's got gunfights, poker games, stagecoaches... all the good stuff!"

Dad looked at me.

"How about it, Buster?" he said. "Want to watch with me?"

Dad rubbed the spot on the couch next to him.

Maybe I should, I thought. It had been ages since I'd spent any real time with Dad. He watched so many westerns that I barely saw him anymore—just his face, smiling in the glow of the TV screen as gunshots ricocheted.

And there was something else.

Sure, Dad's westerns were silly—the swaggering sheriffs, the ladies in lacy dresses, the snarling bad guys. But something about westerns just felt... right. The good guys always won. The bad guys always lost.

Westerns were simple. And I could sit there and watch them with Dad, like a little girl again. I even kind of liked Dad's nicknames for me.

While I was thinking about all this, Dad patted the

couch next to him and sent up another poof-cloud of dust. I pictured the things in that dust—spores, bacteria, mold.

The hair on my arms rose.

"Uh, no thanks," I said to Dad. "Not tonight. Too much homework."

Dad's face fell, but then a fistfight in a saloon broke out on the TV, and just like that, he was back into his movie.

I headed up to my room.

An hour later, when I passed Dad on my way to the kitchen for a snack, I noticed something. He'd settled lower into the couch, and the cushions had kind of folded in around his legs and sides.

"Hey, Dad," I said, leaning in from the hallway. "You're sinking."

He didn't look up. He just kept watching John Wayne. He did answer me, though.

"Yeah, Bandit," he said. "That's how these good couches are. They practically wrap you up in their cushions. It's luxurious." He flashed his smile.

When I walked by a half hour later, he'd sunk even lower. His waist and thighs were buried in the couch like they'd been swallowed by the pillowy cushions.

"Um, Dad. Are you sure that's normal?" I asked. Hoofbeats rang out from the TV.

"Perfectly normal," he said, and he turned up the TV. "I've never been so cozy." Still, he seemed to be squirming. I thought of quicksand.

"You should get up," I said. "Dad, you should really get up."

"Sure thing, Heidi-o," he said. "Give me just a second." He wriggled a little, but he stayed put, glued to the TV. He started reciting the movie right along with John Wayne.

The next time I checked on him, twenty minutes later, he'd disappeared up to his armpits. He was just shoulders and a head and a big Stetson hat, jutting out of the center couch cushion, but his smile still beamed, and his eyes were still fixed on the TV.

From the hallway, I called to him.

"You've got to get out of there, Dad," I said. "You've just got to."

He wriggled around again, but nothing happened. Finally I marched into the room, grabbed his shoulders, and pulled. I leaned with all my weight, but it didn't help. He sank even lower.

Panicking, I ran to the garage and grabbed a rope, thinking I could tie him up like a rodeo calf and pull. But when I burst back into the TV room, all I could see was Dad's face, John Wayne reflected in his rusty-brown eyes.

I yelled for Mom. She came into the room just in time to see Dad's big smile—the last part of him—sink beneath the billowy cushions and vanish. As he went under, his hat settled onto the middle couch cushion.

Everything went quiet. Even the movie on the TV seemed to go silent.

"Dad?" I said. "Are you there?"

I poked the couch with a finger. I waited. Mom and I slapped the cushions and prodded the folds of the couch with broom handles. We tore the cushions off and felt into the couch's crevices like you would for loose change.

But it didn't make any difference.

He was gone.

<hr/>

We kept the couch for three months. We didn't sit on it. Not even once. We just left it there, in the TV room, hoping Dad would climb out.

Sometimes I wonder what would have happened if I'd plopped down on the couch with him that night and watched *Rio Bravo* by his side.

Would the couch have swallowed me, too? Or would I have been able to save him?

After a while, looking at the couch made us miss Dad too much. So one November morning, Mom and I moved it out to the curb. It wasn't easy. We had to nudge and slide and push and grunt.

But eventually we muscled it out next to a fire hydrant.

Panting, I stood by the couch for a quiet minute, and I thought of some of Dad's nicknames for me.

Tex. Bronco. Lefty.

Then I trudged back inside.

The couch didn't stay there long. Like I said, people in our neighborhood did this kind of thing all the time, and after a few minutes, when I checked through the window, the couch was gone.

SORRY, FROGGY

BRADY stuffed the last of his pizza bomb into his mouth.

"Blech," said Julie Simmons from across the lunchroom table. "You eat like a caveman."

Brady opened his mouth, leaned forward, and showed Julie his half-chewed food—a mash of crust and pepperoni and cheese. Julie was always going on about blue whales and lost puppies. Making her look at a mouthful of meat was just what she deserved.

"You're disgusting," Julie said. She rolled her eyes.

Brady didn't care what Julie thought. Pizza bombs were the best things they made in the cafeteria. You couldn't help but wolf them down. Julie Simmons, the Veggiesaurus rex, would never understand that because she only ate things like tofu and arugula. The weirdo.

Besides, Brady wanted to get through with lunch as fast as he could. After lunch came Biology, and today was the day he'd longed for since the first day of seventh grade.

He was finally—*finally!*—going to dissect a frog.

That was the whole reason he'd taken Biology in the first place—to dissect things. When he'd signed up, he'd imagined himself in a white lab coat and stretchy rubber gloves cutting out lungs and eyeballs and hearts and laying them neatly on a table. He'd figured it'd be a bit like being a mad scientist.

But so far, Biology hadn't been anything like mad science. It had just been . . . well . . . science.

They were two months into the school year, and he hadn't gotten to dissect anything. Instead, he'd read long chapters from a thick-spined book called *Life and You* (which was filled with impossible-to-pronounce words and not nearly enough pictures). And he'd listened to Mr. Gough's mind-numbing lectures on circulatory systems, ecosystems, and a dozen other kinds of systems (which always made Brady's eyes droop). And he'd even written three essays and taken two tests (on which he'd earned a C and a C minus).

But all that was about to change. Because today was mad science day. Everyone was talking about it.

"I just don't see what it accomplishes," said Julie Simmons to anyone at the lunch table who would listen, "cutting up those frogs just so we can learn some dumb lesson. I mean, it's cruel."

Brady snorted.

Of course Julie would whine about the frogs. When she walked home from school, she sometimes stopped and talked to the squirrels and birds—"Oh, good morning, Mr. Squirrel. Are you gathering a lot of nuts today?" Brady had seen her do it. And last year when a huge spider crept down the whiteboard in Ms. Baker's class, instead of just letting Brady squash it, Julie had coaxed it onto a blank sheet of paper and released it out the window.

Yep. A definite weirdo.

"I think I'll fake sick," she went on, "to see if I can get out of it."

Brady snorted again, louder this time, hoping she'd hear.

"You don't have the guts to fake sick," he said, and he knew it was true. Julie might have been an animal-loving tree hugger, but she was also a classic Goody Two-Shoes. She'd do anything to get an A. She wouldn't fake sick if her life depended on it.

Julie, Brady figured, was getting exactly the dilemma she deserved. She could dissect a frog and get an A, or she could skip the dissection and get an F. He bet it was the kind of predicament that gave her nightmares.

Brady smiled.

With five minutes still left in the lunch break, he cleared his tray and bolted to the classroom. He was the first one there besides Mr. Gough, who actually was wearing a white lab coat. The old teacher was getting things ready, pulling silver trays out of the supply closet and laying them on the students' desks. The trays were about the size of the rect-angular cakes his mom sometimes baked, and in each tray was a scalpel with a small pointy blade and a pair of white stretchy gloves. Best of all, right in the center of each tray lay a grayish dead frog. The frogs, about the size of hockey pucks, looked stiff and shriveled.

"Sweet," Brady whispered to himself.

That was when the smell hit him, like chemical pickles.

Mr. Gough had warned the students about it the day before. "Formaldehyde is a compound used to preserve the frogs," he'd told them. "It's pretty strong."

Brady took his seat. His eyes watered and his nostrils flared. He rubbed his eyes and breathed the smell away.

Mr. Gough placed a tray in front of him.

His frog lay belly-up, and the soft skin of its underbelly gleamed, reflecting the fluorescent classroom lights.

Brady couldn't believe it. Soon he'd get to hold the thing in his hands. He'd get to poke it, wriggle it, dangle it over some girl's head (preferably Julie Simmons, who sat next to him, a fact he hated most days—but one that would come in handy today). And, even better, he would get to slice the frog open, making a straight cut up its chest like Mr. Gough had taught. He'd get to fold back its skin, pluck out its tiny heart, and roll it, like a marble, between his fingers.

He shifted a little in his chair. He couldn't wait. Mad scientist time was coming.

Nothing, he thought, *can ruin this.*

Just then, Julie Simmons walked in.

"Eww," Julie said, taking her seat next to Brady. She plugged her nose, and her face went the color of cooked pasta. "This smells awful."

Brady rolled his eyes.

She made a pouty face at the dead frog in her tray. "Ohhh," she said. "The poor thing."

Ugh, Brady thought. He couldn't wait to "accidentally" splatter frog guts on her.

The bell rang, but instead of letting his students get to it, Mr. Gough launched into a droning lecture. He went over all the instructions and warnings he'd covered the day before, and he reminded the class four times that the scalpels in their trays were "really sharp."

Wrap it up, Brady thought.

Finally Mr. Gough wound down and said, "You may begin."

Brady snapped on his rubber gloves.

Julie's hand shot up. "Mr. Gough," she said. "I don't think we should do this."

Brady sighed.

"And why is that?" Mr. Gough said.

"Because it's cruel," Julie said. "These frogs are innocent."

Innocent? Such a weirdo.

Mr. Gough rubbed his chin. "Julie," he said, "I know this is hard for you. But the frogs won't feel a thing. I promise. Besides, if you don't dissect the frog, it will have died for nothing. And you won't get credit for the assignment."

Julie sank in her chair.

Brady smiled. He picked up his scalpel. *Take that*, he thought.

"But . . ."—Julie pointed at the frog in her tray—"my frog's eyes are open. I can't dissect something that's looking at me. It's just . . . wrong."

Brady leaned over. Julie was right. Her frog's eyes were

open. So were the eyes on his frog. They shone wet and glassy and dark.

"Julie." Mr. Gough sighed. "The frog isn't looking at you. It isn't watching, and it can't see a thing. Okay?" He tapped his watch. "You need to get started."

With that, Mr. Gough turned away.

"Yeah," Brady whispered to Julie. "Toughen up."

She shot him a look. "How would you like it," she said, "if you were the one in the tray?" Her eyes flared. A heat seemed to come from them.

"I wouldn't mind a bit," he said, "because then I wouldn't be talking to you."

Julie frowned.

"We'll see," she said, and her eyes flared again. She shot him a wild-eyed look Brady had never seen before—not in all the years he'd known her, since first grade. Her pupils seemed to shrink to a fine point and then flare back up to their normal size.

So weird.

Brady ignored her and pushed up his sleeves. Leave it to stupid Julie Simmons to make the one good day in Biology class less fun. Sure, the frogs' eyes were open, but so what? It wasn't like their eyes were working. Like Mr. Gough said, the frogs were dead.

Dead, dead, dead.

To prove the point, Brady brought his scalpel close to the frog's eye. He formed a plan. He would call Julie's name, and when she looked, he'd jab the blade into the frog's pupil. That'd teach her. And her reaction would be priceless. She'd probably scream. She might even gag.

His scalpel blade shone as it gently brushed the frog's eye, but before he could call Julie's name and jab, his own eye started to itch, like something was in it, an eyelash or a bit of dust.

He blinked and squinted, but the itch didn't go away. He dropped his scalpel, rubbed his eye with his wrist, and after a few seconds, the itch finally faded.

Next to him, Julie slowly pulled on her gloves and picked up her scalpel.

"Sorry, froggy," she said into her tray. "I have to do this." With a wince and one eye closed, she made her first incision.

Brady clicked his tongue at her. *Weirdo, weirdo, weirdo.*

He brought his own scalpel down to his frog's chest, pressing it into the soft flesh of the frog's lower belly. He broke the skin, and an ooze of clear liquid seeped out. Slowly, he sliced a straight line up to the neck.

Suddenly he felt a prickle on his own stomach and a hard scratch, like a sharp fingernail running up his sternum.

He dropped his scalpel. It clattered noisily onto the tray, and he stood, pushing his chair back with a loud *screech*.

He rubbed his chest.

Heartburn, he told himself. The pizza bombs. He'd eaten too fast. He'd been too excited about Biology class, and now his insides were shifting. That was what he was feeling.

Normal, everyday heartburn. From too much pepperoni and sausage. That was all.

"Are you okay?" Julie said, and it seemed for a second that she smiled. "You look like you might be sick."

"I'm fine," he said.

"Did someone say 'sick'?" Mr. Gough walked over. "Kids have thrown up doing this before. If you need a break, Brady, that's fine."

A few kids around him snickered. "Brady's going to puke," someone whispered.

"I'm okay," Brady said loudly. He picked up his scalpel. "I'm alright."

He went back to work. Slowly, he peeled open his frog's chest, and the frog's organs came into view—the liver, the intestines. The heartburn in his own chest swelled and spread, and he began to sweat from it, just a little. Why did this have to happen today?

Next to him Julie smiled again.

"What are you so happy about?" he said, pressing a gloved hand to his chest. "I thought you hated this assignment."

She didn't answer, but her smile stayed plastered on her face.

Brady tried to remember what to do next. Remove the liver? The lungs? The pain in his own chest kept swelling, and it began to cloud his mind. Everything was foggy. A bead of sweat trickled down his forehead. He poked his scalpel into the open chest cavity and shifted the liver and lungs.

His own chest rumbled. His breath caught in his throat. Next to him, Julie stopped working.

"Having problems?" she said.

He didn't answer.

He shifted the frog's organs again and grimaced. Then he saw it—the heart. He wanted it. He wanted to be the mad scientist. Julie Simmons and his stupid heartburn were ruining everything, but now he'd roll the heart between his fingers. He'd hold it in front of Julie's face. That would wipe her smile away. Maybe he'd even press the heart into her cheek or toss it into her hair. He gripped his scalpel and, pushing through the pain in his chest, jabbed the blade down, like a spear.

He hit the frog's heart right in the center.

The pain in his chest exploded.

He fell to the ground and couldn't breathe. He tried to scream, but nothing came out. Julie stood above him, and he pointed up to his tray. The scalpel in the frog's chest stuck up like a small flag. He knew what was happening. He needed Julie to get the scalpel, to take it from the frog's heart.

Take it out! he tried to tell her. But the words wouldn't come. He tried to stand, but his legs didn't work either.

Suddenly there was buzzing all around him, and Mr. Gough was pushing students away and shouting, "Get back! Give him air!" and after a few seconds, "Call the nurse."

Then everything became fuzzy and muffled, like he was underwater.

"I don't know what happened," he heard Julie saying, and her words seemed to be coming from far away. "He just fell down and grabbed his chest."

And then the world darkened, and he passed out from the pain.

———

It took the paramedics eleven minutes to arrive. When they did, they loaded Brady onto a stretcher and wheeled him quickly out of the classroom.

"We'll take good care of him," one burly paramedic called as they pushed Brady out the door.

The second he was gone, the classroom buzzed.

"He wouldn't stop twitching," said a student in the back.

"I've never seen a face like that," said another.

"He kept grabbing at his chest," said a girl who sat up front. "Can kids have heart attacks?"

Finally Mr. Gough clapped his hands. "I'm sure Brady will be fine," he said, and then he told the students to return to their work.

Julie raised her hand. "Can I clean up Brady's desk for him?" she asked. "It's the least I could do."

Mr. Gough nodded. "Of course, Julie," he said. "That's very kind."

Julie picked up Brady's tray. The scalpel stuck out of his frog's chest at a funny angle, like a javelin in the ground.

"Sorry, froggy," Julie whispered, "but he needs to learn."

And she left the scalpel in the frog's heart.

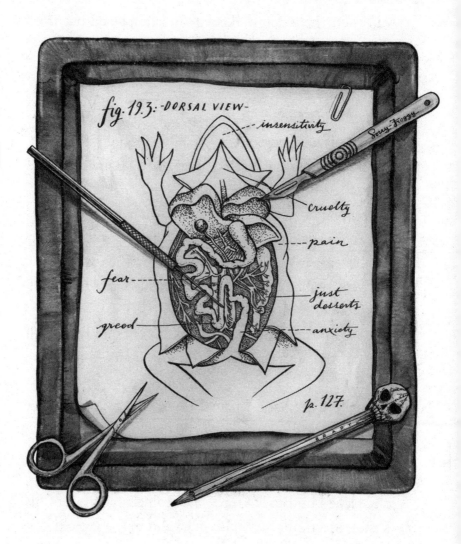

She covered the tray with a sheet of plastic that Mr. Gough brought her. Then she slid the whole thing into the supply closet.

She'd remove the scalpel, she told herself, when the time was right. She just couldn't bring herself to leave it in the poor frog's heart forever.

But Brady was a stubborn boy. She closed the supply closet and returned to her seat, where she gently stroked her own half-dissected frog. It would take him days—maybe weeks—to learn his lesson.

The weirdo.

Staring Contest

L IVVY couldn't sleep. Again.

Even though she and her dad had lived in the creaky old house for nearly a month, everything about it—from the ugly windows that let in the nighttime sounds to the wood floors that squeaked even when no one was stepping on them—felt wrong.

"This house is a hundred and twelve years old," her dad had told her when they'd started hauling in their boxes. "That makes it the oldest member of our family."

Well, if this house is family, she'd thought, catching the old-house scent for the first time, dusty and a bit damp, like a barn, *then it's a creepy, weird uncle.*

And creepy was right.

Livvy smoothed her covers.

That first day, when she'd set foot inside the house carrying a box of art supplies, a cold shiver ran down Livvy's back, like someone had just traced a fingernail along her spine.

And it wasn't only the old smell or the way the house looked that gave Livvy the shivers, though the faded yellow wallpaper hanging in peeled strips and the cracks that spiderwebbed across the front window certainly didn't help.

It was a feeling like the one she got whenever she had to walk through a metal detector at an airport. Like something was examining her to her core. It gave her goose bumps. And those goose bumps rose on her arms every single time she walked into the house.

Every. Single. Time.

It was like knowing someone was filming her but not knowing where the camera was. Lately, she'd even started imagining eyes all over the house, as if the walls themselves were watching her. The first eye she'd seen had been in a crack in a low corner of her bathroom mirror. That crack had a round divot at its center, like the mirror had been struck by something, and the breaks that circled the divot gave the crack a disturbing, wide-eyed shape.

The next eye Livvy found had been in the wood grain of a kitchen cabinet. It was just an eye-shaped knot, Livvy knew, but as she ate her cereal, Livvy could feel it peering at her, constant and unblinking.

Over the last few weeks, she'd even seen eye shapes in cobwebs. New webs seemed to show up all the time—the house had a real spider problem—and whenever Livvy found a new web, it always had an eye-shaped tangle of strings at its center.

Of course Livvy knew these eyes were just the result of her artistic imagination. She'd been reminding herself of that for weeks.

The house couldn't be watching her.

But thinking of the eyes made her shiver under her covers. She pulled her blanket up to her chin.

"Just close your eyes," she told herself. "Go to sleep."

Her dad's snores murmured into her room, audible through the house's thin walls, and she tried breathing in sync with him.

She counted five breaths. Then ten breaths. Then twenty.

It didn't help. How could he just sleep in this house so easily?

He didn't seem to get that this house wasn't ... right.

"What an adventure," he'd said brightly that first day as he'd turned on the sink and no water had come out.

He hadn't seemed bothered by anything—not by the house's smell or its creaks or even the layer of dust they'd spent two whole days clearing away. For him, the house was a hobby. Since moving in, he'd ripped out all the wallpaper and replaced the kitchen sink. He'd straightened the crooked front door and installed a new front window. He'd even put up shiny new rain gutters.

He whistled while he did all this, as if being a handyman was his new calling, as if moving two hundred miles to a new job and a new life was the best thing that had ever happened to him.

She sighed, listened to his snoring, and counted twenty more of her own breaths. Then thirty. Then fifty.

It had all started two months ago, when he'd sat her down at the kitchen table one night after dinner. He told her he was tired of being a doctor in a big city, and he said that he needed to be in a small town where *doctors still knew their patients' names*, and *bumped into them at the grocery store*.

Then he laid out his plan and showed her a picture of their new house.

This house.

And just like that, everything changed. One morning, not long after moving in, she'd pointed out to him how the knot in the kitchen cabinet looked kind of like an eye, but he'd only tilted his head and squinted.

"Huh," he'd said. "That's pretty cool."

Pretty cool. Livvy stopped counting her breaths. *Well, the house still smells like the inside of an old suitcase.* She straightened her covers realizing the house would probably always smell terrible, no matter how many repairs her dad made.

"Give it time," her dad had said. "You'll warm up to the old girl."

The old girl. That's what he called the house—like it was a living, breathing thing.

Well, she'd given it time. It had been almost a month. And Livvy wasn't warming up to *the old girl*—not by one single degree.

"Stupid house," she said out loud, and just then the house made a sound—a kind of moaning, like the roof beams above her were settling.

She sat up in bed. The sound faded, so she fluffed her pillow a few times and flopped back onto it.

She narrowed her eyes at the plaster ceiling, where the settling, moaning noise had come from.

She took in a sharp breath. She shivered and let out a little wince.

Because there was another eye—a perfect plaster eye, opened wide, looking straight down at Livvy from her bedroom ceiling. The eye's shape was so obvious, so clear, she was amazed she hadn't noticed it before. Its lines were sharp. Its pupil, a perfect circle. She didn't see how she could possibly have missed it for the last month. This eye was huge, larger than a football, and it was right above her, staring down, without blinking.

She shuddered.

The feeling she'd had, of being constantly watched, filled her chest. For the hundredth time since moving in, her neck prickled.

"Stupid house," she said again.

She breathed. She counted ten more breaths. She tried to calm down.

It's just a bit of plaster, Livvy told herself. It was a strange accident of how someone had textured the plaster on a ceiling a hundred years ago. One of the splatters just happened to look like an eye. That was all it was—that and her imagination. That was all.

She tried to ignore the eye, but now that she'd seen it, she knew she'd never be able to stop seeing it. Every time she'd lie down in bed, there it would be, this stupid plaster eye hovering over her.

She took a deep breath and pulled her blankets up to her nose.

Maybe, she thought, she could get Dad to scrape the eye off first thing in the morning. Maybe his next project could be retexturing her ceiling. She'd ask him about it at breakfast.

She rolled onto her side. Still, she felt the eye. She thought about dragging her bed to the other side of the room.

She tried to lighten the mood by making a face at the eye.

"Staring contest," she said, remembering the game she had played when she was younger. She hoped speaking out loud would chase the eeriness of the moment away, so she opened her eyes, glared at the ceiling, and whispered, "Ready! Go!"

The eye seemed to shift and open itself slightly wider.

It must be the light, Livvy told herself. The moon, she figured, coming out from behind a cloud and shining through her window. Still, she tried not to blink.

After a few seconds, her eyes began to water.

She held her stare, but when the burning became too much, she blinked.

When she opened her eyes, the ceiling seemed suddenly lower, as if it had dropped a few inches, maybe half a foot closer to her face during the split second her eyes had been closed.

She shook herself. *The moonlight*, she told herself again. *Playing tricks.*

She looked at the eye.

"Rematch," she said.

She stared for a minute, and again her tired eyes watered and burned. When she blinked and opened them, the room seemed shorter once more—the eye, a little nearer.

It's nothing, she told herself. She was just missing her old house, the one back in the city. It had high ceilings, so her new ceiling seemed lower by comparison. That was all.

Outside the wind whipped, and the window rattled.

She focused on the eye once more. When she blinked this time, the eye seemed bigger and nearer than it had been just seconds before.

It's because I haven't been sleeping well, she told herself. Missed sleep was making her see things.

But when she blinked yet again, she wondered if the crummy house could actually be falling down. Sagging under the weight of its age in the strong wind.

After two more blinks, she simply couldn't deny it anymore.

The ceiling was dropping. Bit by bit. Every time she blinked. She started to feel smothered under her covers.

"Stay up there," she whispered, speaking to the plaster eye. "Please." She kept her eyes open for as long as she could, but they started to water and burn. She held them open, looking deep into the ceiling for longer than she thought possible.

But when the burning became too much, she blinked.

Now the eye was so close that she could have stretched up a hand and touched it.

And she knew the truth.

The house was out to get her. Maybe it had been from the very first day.

Her neck and shoulders shivered. When she blinked again, the ceiling was just a foot above her face, hovering like a wrecking ball. She tried to move, to slink out of bed and run for her father, but the eye seemed to have her frozen, plastered against her mattress.

"Dad," she called out. But his snoring didn't change.

She fought to keep her eyes open.

"Dad," she called again, louder. She waited...

Her vision blurred, and though she tried, the burning in her eyes became too much, and she blinked, and the eye was so close now. Just inches above the tip of her nose.

Just there.

If she blinked once more, what would happen? Would the ceiling smother her? Crush her? Or would the eye swallow her up? Would she get sucked into it and become a part of this sagging house?

Dad, she tried to call, but she couldn't even speak anymore. She was quaking, shivering, and the eye seemed to be boring into her.

Would she end up just a shape, another eye somewhere on a baseboard or window or wall? What if all the eyes she'd seen had belonged to people once, actual people this house had devoured?

The thought made her breathe short panting breaths.

She strained her eyes, opening them as wide as she could. They burned.

The plaster eye, larger than her head, hung just over her. It peered into her. Her eyes bulged and ached. She fought through the pain that welled up, and tears spilled onto her cheeks. But she was going to blink. She could feel it.

No, she thought. *Please, no.*

She put all her energy into keeping her eyes open. She couldn't last forever, she knew, but she needed to try. She looked deep into the plaster eye, and her eyelids quivered.

Her breathing grew short.

She strained with everything she had.

She tried counting her breaths. Ten breaths. Fifteen. Twenty.

But in the end, it was no use.

She blinked.

THE SHADOW CURSE

THE SHADOW CURSE

WHEN he walked into English class, Mason was sweating and his fingers felt hot. Even his shadow at his feet looked nervous.

The problem was his book report.

He hadn't finished it. More accurately, he hadn't *started* it. Though he'd had more than a month to work on it, he hadn't even chosen a book.

He shook out his hands. He tried to breathe. He had to think. To think, to think, to think.

Five weeks earlier, Mr. Williams had passed out the book-report assignment sheets, copied on bright blue paper. The deadline—April 23—had been printed in a large, bold font at the top.

April 23 is forever away, Mason had thought, and he'd stuffed the sheet into his binder. He'd seen the sheet occasionally since then, its blue edges peeking out from behind white worksheets and graded assignments. But he'd put off the book report. Then he'd put it off some more. And finally he'd forgotten about it completely.

That was, until two minutes ago, when Derek Smithers passed him in the hallway. Derek had been wearing a pirate hat and an eye patch, and he'd been leaning on a crutch. A toy musket hung at his hip.

"Who are you supposed to be?" Mason smirked. Mason would never have dressed up for a school project, not even as a pirate.

"I'm Long John Silver," Derek said, "from *Treasure Island*. It's for the book report."

Mason's eyes widened.

"The book report," Mason repeated slowly. His lungs seemed to drop a few inches in his chest. *Oh, no*, he thought. *No, no, no.*

Now Mason settled into his desk and checked the clock. There had to be a way out of this. There just had to be. After all, he'd talked his way out of assignments before. Last month, Mason had forgotten about the science fair, so he'd told Mrs. Watkins his grandmother had broken her hip, and she'd given him a week extension. And last year, at the end of fifth grade, he'd completely spaced on a Social Studies report, so he'd told Ms. Holland his father had been dealing with a bad case of gout. Mason wasn't even sure what gout was—he'd heard the word on one of those drug commercials—but Ms. Holland had said she was sorry and given Mason three extra days.

So quickly, Mason began filing through the list of excuses in his head.

He could tell Mr. Williams that his dog had just died, that just yesterday, his dog...Shem...a bull terrier, had chased a ball into the street and been hit by...a blue Chevy Impala. Details, Mason knew, were the key to a good lie. Bull terriers, blue Chevy Impalas—these things made a difference.

But Mason had never owned a dog, and some of the kids in class knew this. If the truth about his "bull terrier" got out, then where would he be?

He shook his head and tried again.

He could say that a blue Chevy Impala had hit…him. He could say the car had knocked him down and totaled his bike and that a policeman had come to investigate— a policeman named Officer McCully—and that, luckily, Mason had only sprained his ankle.

But he wasn't injured at all. He shook his head. He had no scrapes or bruises, and he didn't think he could fake a serious injury. Besides, people had already seen him walking around, healthy and strong. He couldn't suddenly develop a limp.

"Think," he whispered. He rapped his fingers on his desk. "Come on, Mason. Think."

In just two minutes, the bell would ring, and Mr. Williams would call Mason's name first, like he always did. It was the curse of having the last name *Adams*. Oh, how he envied kids with last names like *Saunders* or *Melton* or *Nelson*, kids who showed up halfway down the roll. He didn't even like to think about *Ruby Zakowski*, who'd probably never had to go first at anything in her life.

Mason slumped forward and put his forehead in his hands. What was he going to do? He needed more time. Just then, Derek, the one-legged pirate, tottered into the room on his crutch, and more kids trickled in behind him. Diego

Diaz carried a poster map of Narnia. Suzy Penker wore *Alice in Wonderland* finger puppets. Steve Perkins held a tray of magic wand pretzel sticks.

You've had more than a month, Mason told himself. *A month!* He should have been able to think of something.

The bell rang, and Mason shook his head.

Cursed, he thought. *I'm cursed.*

Mr. Williams stood up.

"Mason Adams," he called, just as Mason had expected. "Please stand and deliver your report." The words sounded fuzzy to Mason, like they were coming at him through a pillow.

"Um," he said, not standing up. "There's been a little problem."

Mr. Williams raised his bushy eyebrows. "A problem?" he said. A few kids snickered.

It was now or never, Mason knew. Tell the right story or go down in flames.

"It was...my mom," Mason said, scrambling for an idea. The class fell quiet. "She, uh, wanted to read my book because...because I told her how great it was, so she took it into the bathroom with her, and somehow...dropped it in... the toilet." His classmates snickered some more. "She said she'd get me another copy. But she didn't. So I didn't get to finish it."

Even to Mason, the story sounded pretty lame.

Cursed, he thought.

"Your mom dropped your book in the toilet?" Mr. Williams said.

More laughter.

"Yeah," Mason said, trying to sound annoyed. "*Ker-plop*. And she forgot to get me another copy like she said she would."

Mr. Williams seemed to be thinking. He lifted a pen out of his shirt pocket and clicked it a few times.

"How much of the book did you read before your mother, shall we say, damaged it?"

A red flag went up in Mason's mind. If he said he hadn't read much of the book, Mr. Williams would ask why he didn't just choose another one. But if he said he'd read a lot, Mr. Williams would probably ask him questions about it.

"I read about half," Mason said, settling on what he thought was the safest answer.

"Well," said Mr. Williams, tapping his pen on his clipboard. "Please stand and tell us about the first half of this toilet-ruined book."

There was nothing else to do, so Mason trudged his way to the front of the classroom. The fluorescent lights above him buzzed, and below him, his squat, dark shadow slid along the carpet. *Cursed*, he told himself. Mike Truncheon in the front row stretched a leg and tried to trip Mason as he passed, and a few kids giggled.

Mason breathed slowly. He avoided eye contact with anyone in the room, choosing instead to look down at his gloomy shadow.

"My book..." he said in what he hoped was a confident,

class-presentation voice, and then a thought flickered in his head. It had something to do with his shadow, just there wavering on the carpet. The thought was just below the surface, but it was rising like a submarine. An idea was coming. He could feel it.

He waited for it. His shadow swayed slowly on the tan carpet below, and the idea came closer...closer. Steve Perkins coughed.

"My book," he started again, "that my mom destroyed in the most horrifying of ways...was called...*The Shadow Curse*."

Mason smiled. The idea had arrived. It was still raw. But there was hope. Mason stood up a little straighter.

"*The Shadow Curse*," Mr. Williams repeated from the back of the room with his raised bushy eyebrows. "Never heard of it."

"Well," Mason said, "it's really good."

"Go on," Mr. Williams said, and he leaned one shoulder against the back wall. Mason couldn't be sure, but it seemed like Mr. Williams was smiling, as if he was looking forward to watching Mason squirm.

I guess we'll see about that, Mason thought, slightly more confident now that the idea was taking shape.

"*The Shadow Curse*," Mason said, "is about a boy named Morton."

"Morton?" Suzy Penker said from the second row. "What kind of name is Morton?"

Mason pointed at Suzy. "Morton is an awesome name," he said. "The best name ever." A few of his classmates rolled their eyes. This wasn't starting like he'd hoped.

He went on. "Morton is just a normal kid living a normal life."

Mike Truncheon in the front row faked a yawn, but the idea came into clearer focus and Mason spoke faster.

"Which is why Morton's shadow hates him so much."

"His shadow?" said Ruby Zakowski.

"Yes, his shadow," Mason said. He pointed to his own shadow below him. "See, Morton does normal kid things. He goes to school, and he goes shopping with his mom, and he hangs out with his friends, and the shadow thinks all of this is stupid and boring."

"The shadow's got a point," said Mike Truncheon.

"So wherever Morton goes, his shadow has to go, too. Whatever Morton does, his shadow has to do." Mason walked across the front of the classroom and waved a hand at his own shadow as it followed.

"The shadow might want to go outside and slither over the grass," Mason went on, "but it can't because Morton goes to Math class. Or the shadow might want to keep watching baseball, but Morton will change the channel to some old movie instead. Eventually the shadow gets really mad. He feels like Morton is his personal little prison."

A few kids leaned sideways in their desks and looked down at their own shadows. Mason kept going.

"Actually," said Mason, "that's one of the chapter titles in the book—'Morton Is a Prison.' It's chapter 4, I think. So one day the shadow decides to get rid of Morton."

"Get rid of him?" said Suzy Penker.

Mason paused. Then he lowered his voice.

"By killing him," he said. He drew a finger across his neck.

"Whoa," said Billy Lewis in the back. "That's dark."

"But then won't the shadow die, too?" This came from Suzy Penker.

"Well, it might," Mason said. "But the shadow doesn't think so. It's a risk the shadow is willing to take. Once Morton's out of the way, the shadow thinks it'll be able to fly wherever it wants."

Mason paused for a few seconds. He let the story sink in.

"How?" said Billy Lewis. "How's the shadow going to kill Morton?"

Mason needed another few seconds to think, so he waited. He looked at his own shadow below. It swayed from side to side, and Mason realized he was swaying, too. He stopped.

"The shadow decides to smother Morton's heart," Mason finally said. "The shadow's connected to Morton's body at his feet, so the shadow decides to invade Morton's body and work its way up his legs and chest to his heart, where the shadow plans to crush it and stop it beating forever."

"Evil," said Mike Truncheon. "I like it."

"The problem," Mason went on, "is that whenever the shadow starts to invade Morton's body, Morton gets all tingly—like, he gets a pins-and-needles feeling in his feet and legs where the shadow is moving in."

"I've felt that," said Suzy Penker. "In my feet. All the time."

"Yeah," said Mason. "But when Morton feels this, like when he's watching TV or sitting at a desk, he jumps up or wiggles his feet or stomps, and the shadow has to retreat."

The class grew quiet. Mr. Williams cocked his head to one side. *This is good*, Mason thought. *This is really good.* Mason straightened his posture. His shadow shifted under the fluorescent classroom lights.

He leaned forward and lowered his voice.

"Well, one night, when Morton gets in bed, Morton's shadow is just lying there like always, and it can hear Morton's heart beating away—*thu-thump, thu-thump, thu-thump.*" Mason patted a heartbeat rhythm on his chest with one hand. "So the shadow creeps up Morton's body, and Morton's toes and feet start to tingle."

Mason kept the heartbeat pats going on his chest. He let the class listen. *Thu-thump. Thu-thump.*

"Morton thinks his feet are falling asleep, so he just lies there. Then his legs begin to tingle, all the way up to his knees."

Mason's hand kept moving, tapping out the heartbeat rhythm on his chest. *Thu-thump.* Suzy Penker began tapping her foot to it.

"But Morton ignores the tingling and falls asleep. The

tingling moves up past his waist and into his ribs, and the shadow is so excited because if it can just creep up a few more inches, it'll reach Morton's beating heart." Mason took a half step forward. His shadow followed. His hand continued to thump on his chest.

He lowered his voice to a near whisper and spoke barely loud enough to be heard. "The shadow is just three inches from Morton's heart. Then two inches. Then one."

Mason patted. *Thu-thump*. The wall clock ticked.

"Finally the shadow touches Morton's heart, and it starts to squeeze."

Mason stopped patting his chest. He stopped speaking.

"So what happens next?" asked Derek Smithers, the pirate.

The students sat perfectly still, and Mr. Williams in the back leaned forward slightly.

Mason had them. He had them all.

So it was time to stop.

"Well, that's just it," Mason said. "That's as far as I got when my mom ... well ... *ker-plop*."

The class groaned.

"So you had to stop reading where Morton was being killed?" said Suzy Penker.

"By his own shadow?" said Mike Truncheon.

"And you can't even tell us if he survives?" said Derek Smithers. "You didn't skip ahead to check?"

"Hey," Mason said. "How do you think I feel? Besides, *The*

Shadow Curse was a library book, and my mom's going to make me pay for it."

As soon as he'd said this last part, he knew he'd gone too far, but no one questioned him. None of them even tilted their heads. They were sitting at their desks, thinking. Mike Truncheon in the front row stamped his left foot three times and flexed his toes. Ruby Zakowski looked down at the shadow by her desk.

"Well," said Mr. Williams. He was scratching something onto his clipboard. "That was interesting, Mason. Quite interesting."

"Yeah, I'm sorry I can't tell you how it ended," Mason said as he walked back to his seat. "I really am."

No one spoke.

Mason settled calmly into his desk.

"How much of this book did you say you read?" Mr. Williams asked, fidgeting with his pen.

"About half," Mason answered.

Mr. Williams tapped his pen on his clipboard. "Well," he said. "I'll give you half credit now, and when you finish the book I'll give you the rest of the points."

"Thank you," Mason said. "That's really fair, Mr. Williams. Thanks a lot."

Mason's chest puffed out. He couldn't believe it. He'd pulled it off! He'd received points without even cracking a book. He opened his notebook and started doodling while he fought the urge to smile. If he looked too proud, too smug,

he'd give everything away. Suzy Penker and Derek the Pirate were still looking at him, and so was Mr. Williams, so he kept his mouth in an even, unsmiling line. Inside, though, he was practically dancing.

But he shouldn't have been.

Below him, his own shadow darkened.

It had been listening to Mason's story. And it had heard everything.

On the floor, its murky shape pulsed. It moved as if it were made of heavy, dark chains that were connected to Mason—always connected to Mason—at his feet.

And the shadow felt something. A steady, confident heartbeat. *Thu-thump. Thu-thump. Thu-thump.* It was coming from Mason's chest.

With that, the shadow made its choice.

Mason's toes began to tingle.

ACKNOWLEDGMENTS

I must thank, first and forever, my wife, Suzy—who always believed in this book—and my four children, whose words, hopes, and fears run all across these pages. And I must thank my mother, who taught me to love books, and my father, who showed me *The Twilight Zone* before I was quite ready, sparking a lifelong fascination with the weird and the creepy.

I am grateful to a host of friends who read early drafts of this book. They include Steve Stewart, Jason Williams, Jack Harrell, Suzette Kunz, Paula Soper, Avery Baker, Rachel Scoresby, Amber Brubaker, and Brindy McLean. And I'm grateful to my colleagues at BYU-Idaho for their comradery and unfailing support. I'm grateful to former writing teachers, specifically Margaret Blair Young, Janet Peery, and Sheri Reynolds, for their patience and wisdom.

I am deeply indebted to Gary D. Schmidt, a fine writer and an even finer soul, for introducing me to the best agent a new writer could hope for—Rick Margolis. And I am grateful every day for the good people at Holiday House, including my always sensitive and always graceful editor, Sally Morgridge.

I am beyond thrilled that Sarah J. Coleman's name is printed next to mine on the cover of this book. Thank you, Sarah, for such beautifully creepy artwork, and thank you for being unafraid of the dark.

Finally I'm grateful to readers. And to schoolteachers. And to librarians. And to all the children who've ever heard a mysterious creak in the night...and wondered.